I0629939

# I KILL IN PEACE

# ALSO BY HUNTER SHEA

*We Are Always Watching*

*Combustible*

# I KILL IN PEACE

## HUNTER SHEA

# I KILL IN PEACE

*For Jason Brant, a man who fully appreciates horror, writing, and the need for a good drink when discussing the two.*

"But his head no longer sheltered ideas of how things could be and should be on the planet, as opposed to how they really were. There was only one way for the Earth to be, he thought: the way it was."

**—Kurt Vonnegut, Breakfast of Champions**

# THE MESSAGE

# ONE

The instant message warning me that I was about to be fired came just as I was completing a competitive analysis that had taken me the better part of three days. The oblong IM box superimposed itself over my spreadsheet.

It read: **AO: Marcellus is going to call u into his office at 5. He's laying u off.**

The words were shocking, but I didn't know who AO was, so I closed the window, thinking it was meant for someone else. Quadrangle Corp was, after all, a large, multinational company with over thirty thousand employees. Searching the directory for an employee with the initials AO would take up the rest of my day. I did feel sorry for the guy the message was meant for though.

This was a few days after a tropical storm that I'd been told never came to this area of Maine had swept through the county. I mean, the words *tropics* and *Maine* had probably never been uttered in the same sentence before. Our systems were kind of fried, so of course, some wires had gotten crossed.

Concentrating on the price comparison column I needed to finish, the box took center stage again.

**AO: Peter, I'm not kidding. Be prepared.**

The pen dropped from my mouth onto the keyboard.

I wrote back.

**PB: Who is this?**

I sat back in my chair, waiting for a reply. I thought, *if this is Fred messing with me, I'm gonna beat his ass.* Back before we'd been promoted to management, Fred and I spent countless hours pranking one another and our unwitting coworkers. That was two wives—one for each of us—several babies, and four promotions ago. We still dicked around, but outside the office. Since my transfer, I hadn't seen Fred in months. He was a flight away now. Hard to get together for drinks after work or weekend barbecues when the distance between us could be measured in hundreds and hundreds of miles.

Besides, this wasn't funny. I'd just moved to Quad-rangle's Maine office and bought a house, transplanting my family all the way from Florida. It hadn't been an easy move and even though the cost of living was cheap, I was still balls-deep in debt. If I lost my job, I was screwed.

**AO: Someone who's looking out for u.**

Crap. Was it someone from the Miami office who had an in with HR up here?

**PB: If this is a joke, I'm not laughing.**

**AO: Just wanted u to be prepared.**

I stood up, the cubicle wall coming to my chest, and looked around. Everyone was at their desk, working on their computer or on the phone. Was this new guy hazing?

"Very funny," I said.

Several heads turned, waiting for the punch line. Feeling like an idiot, I sat back down in my special lumbar chair. The IM window had somehow closed itself.

It was three o'clock. I still had at least an hour to go on my report. The last hour of the day I'd spend catching up on email. I'd only met our vice president, Marcellus Hanson, twice before. To be kind, I told people he wasn't my cup of tea. He was tall and assertive with a personality that was sometimes bigger than the room. But it didn't take much scratching to find that he was all fluff and no substance. I'd bet my four-year-old could beat him in Scrabble. I had learned his strength though. He knew how to savage a bottom line. So, in lieu of making money, he was the expert at saving it. Ethics be damned in his mission to be the top dog in the kennel of empowered morons. I'd seen his type before. I'd learned long ago to ignore them. I had my own life to worry about. As long as he signed the checks, I couldn't care less what accounts he was shifting around or which pretty project manager he was screwing.

It was my wife, Candy, who'd taught me to pray for people like him. It took a lot of convincing at first, but in the end, she was right. It was easier to pity the guy than rail against him. Kept my blood pressure at a healthy level to boot.

I was down to my last three emails when Marcellus Hanson's secretary called me to come to his office. I looked at the clock.

5:00.

Oh shit.

I checked my computer monitor, hoping for an IM telling me this was all just a joke. My Outlook inbox was the only thing looking back at me.

My hands shook as I took my jacket off the back of my chair. Marcellus's office was on the floor above me. I had to take the stairs because all of the elevators were going down as my (former?) coworkers filed out.

His office was at the end of a short hall. I was out of breath, more from panic than the one flight up the stairs. I had to lean against the wall for a minute to calm down.

Taking several deep breaths, I strode into his office, a fake smile plastered on my face. He had a view of a small pond in the back of the building. It was an unassuming office, but then again, I'd learned that being ostentatious was a trait that would get you drummed out of Bridgton, Maine. If there were any quaint, all-American towns left, this was it.

"Have a seat," Marcellus said. I noticed he hadn't bothered to paint on his own fake smile. His bald head bore several odd creases, as if he'd been in an accident in the past. A thick, bristled mustache kept his upper lip warm. I'd heard him refer to it as his flavor saver.

"I finished that competitive analysis today," I said, hoping he couldn't hear the quaver in my voice. "I'll have everything ready for you in the morning."

He leaned against his desk. "That won't be necessary."

My stomach dropped to my tightening sack.

*Oh my god. It's really happening.*

"Pete, we're going to have to let you go."

Blam! Like a bullet to the heart, he just let it all out at once. I couldn't find any words to retort.

"You know we've had a tough quarter. It's nothing personal, Pete. We just need to trim some headcount. We'll give you three weeks' severance and I'll write a glowing recommendation for you."

"Three weeks' severance?" I said, the words clawing from my throat. I'd been with the company for over a decade and had even relocated to stay with it.

"You're a bright guy. I bet the moment you drop your line in the water, you'll have more fish than you'll know what to do with." He pushed away from the desk, staring at me.

"That...that's it?" I said.

"I'm afraid so," he replied without an ounce of care or contrition. "Now, if you don't mind, I have several other people I need to speak with. Any questions can be brought up with HR. They'll meet you at your desk in a bit."

And with that, I was dismissed. He turned from me to his tablet. I was a ghost to him in less time than it takes to sneeze. I had a hard time getting out of the chair. It was an effort to get my knees to unlock.

I passed Yolanda in the hallway. She was pale and biting her fingernails.

When she saw my face, she grabbed my arm. "Peter, what happened in there?"

"Marcellus just laid me off." Saying it aloud still didn't make it seem real.

"What? You're the best marketing director we've ever had. Oh Jesus, does that mean he's going to let me go too?" Tiny tears sprang from the creases of her eyes.

"I...I don't know. Hopefully not," I stammered,

walking to the stairwell. I liked Yolanda and wanted to help her out, but I couldn't think, couldn't feel.

*How will Candy react? She's going to flip out. I know it.*

There was a cardboard box on my desk. No one from HR was around. It sounded like they were going to have a busy night. Numbly, I started to fill the box with my marketing books, picture frames, doodles from my daughter, and other things I'd brought from home to make my workspace cozy.

*Blung!*

I looked at my computer.

**AO: Are u OK?**

I wasn't sure if I was legally supposed to use my computer, now that I'd been shit-canned.

*What are they gonna do, fire me twice?*

**PB: How did you know?**

**AO: I know a lot. Are u angry?**

**PB: Of course I am. Being fired is one thing. Being fired by a dumbass I don't respect is another.**

**AO: Good.**

**PB: Why is that good?**

**AO: Because u won't feel so bad when u kill him.**

# TWO

I backed away from my laptop as if it were a venomous snake. The IM window blinked out of existence just as Edna from HR arrived at my desk.

"I'm so sorry, Peter," she said. She was young and pretty and had really taken to the empathy courses they'd given her at corporate. I almost believed she cared. "I just need to go over some paperwork with you to make sure you get your severance and we can talk about Cobra insurance and your 401K."

Staring at the blank monitor, all I could muster was, "Yeah, sure."

The rest, until I got to my car with my box under my arm, was a blank.

I dumped the box of my belongings, as well as my severance and benefits folder, into the back seat of my Lumina. The old Chevy had been with me a long time and had borne witness to my highs and lows. This was one for the Lumina's record books.

The drive down Route 302 to my street took less than five minutes. I made sure to catch every light, waiting a little longer at each stop sign. *Where's a slow-footed moose when you need one?* I thought. I dreaded going home. Candy would be devastated, which would, in turn, break me. Maine wasn't exactly humming with job opportunities—not unless you could swing a hammer or had a medical degree. I was shit out of luck on both counts.

I was two blocks away when my phone started buzzing. I pulled over to view the text, hoping it was Candy asking me to stop at the store to pick up something at Hannaford. Hell, I'd go into New Hampshire if I could to avoid the inevitable.

My heart skipped a beat when I saw a text from the mysterious AO.

**AO: Marcellus lives on 189 Alyssa Lane in Wyndham. His wife is in New York visiting family. Be there, tonight, at 9. That's when he leaves to hit the bar.**

"Who the hell are you?" Realizing there was no way the mysterious AO could hear my frantic voice, I texted my confusion.

**AO: Bring your car to the Food Mart lot at 8:30. You'll see a red Mustang with the keys in the ignition. Take it to Marcellus's house. I'll give u further instructions along the way.**

*I wrote back:* **Just leave me alone! I don't want anything to do with Marcellus Hanson. And I'm not getting into any car you leave in a lot. You won't even tell me who you are!!!!!**

The phone stayed silent. I wasn't in the mood for games. Sure, AO had the heads up that I was going to be canned, but this was getting ridiculous. How the hell did he—or she—know my cell number? Was this all some sick game someone in HR was playing on me? Only an HR person would know I was going to be fired and have my personal information. I seethed, dreaming up the lawsuit I was going to slap on the company. I tossed the phone into the box.

*Gotta settle down now. Just step back a little and breathe, I said to myself as I pulled into my driveway.*

When I walked into my house, I was tackled by my daughter Katie. She wrapped herself around my knees. Candy, holding a bowl of steaming mashed potatoes, came over and gave me a quick kiss. Her black hair was in a ponytail and she was wearing her cooking sweats. She still looked gorgeous to me.

"You feel all right?" she asked.

I picked up Katie and held her to my chest. Her chestnut hair smelled like strawberries. The wattage of her little smile could power the International Space Station.

"Yeah, why?"

"You look a little pale," Candy said. She pressed her lips to my forehead. "You don't have a fever. I just saw on the news that there's some terrible virus going around."

"Honey, I'm pale because I'm starving," I lied.

It was an effort getting every bite down, waiting for the moment to tell her. Not with Katie around. A dull throb birthed itself in the center of my skull, getting worse by the minute. After dinner, I loaded the dishwasher, settled Candy and Katie in the family room with the promise of watching *Frozen* for the hundredth time, said I had to go to the bathroom, and threw up everything I'd ever eaten. With each heave, my head felt close to ripping in two.

Was this how my body punished me for lying to Candy?

*Stop being dramatic. It's stress. Plain and simple.*

I'd always been an honest man, sometimes to a fault. Wiping gray goo from my mouth, I flushed my stomach away.

Leaning my head against the cool bowl, an image of a roaring fire flickered against my closed lids. The more I concentrated on the fire, the more my head hurt. My stomach cramped.

*There can't be anything left!*

I opened my eyes, wishing the fire and pain away. It actually seemed to work. My stomach settled down, and I washed myself up. I looked at my reflection in the mirror. My face was the color of Wonder Bread, and my receding hairline was still in retreat. Other than that, I looked the same as always—like a grown version of the kid who got sand kicked in his face by the beach beefcake.

By the time I got back downstairs, my wife and daughter were asleep on the couch. Olaf the snowman was doing his schtick on the TV.

A little chime beeped from my iPad that I kept on the end table. Katie liked to use it to play games. I rarely touched the thing.

Swiping the screen to life, I saw there was a message waiting for me.

I made a dry swallow when I saw it was from AO.

*How the hell does this guy have all my info?*

I opened the email.

**AO: Food Mart in ten minutes. Your family will stay asleep until you come back. Don't worry about them. Worry about yourself.**

I dropped the iPad on the floor, cracking the glass.

*Had this sick fuck somehow drugged Candy and Katie?*

The image of the fire came to me again with a lancing pain in my cranium that brought me to my knees. I tried to breathe through the agony while listening to Princess Elsa sing. I wanted to die.

"I'll go," I muttered, though couldn't recall thinking it.

The pain stopped, but my ears still rang.

I was slow to get up.

I thought about reneging on my assent to do what AO had told me. The instant it flashed in my brain, a bright explosion of rippling agony flittered behind my eyes. My bowels almost completely let go and I wanted to vomit. The pain passed, and I staggered, holding on to the back of the couch.

How was this being done to me? And how was it affecting Candy and Katie? Through my stumbling and heavy groans, they didn't move a muscle. If for nothing else, I had to go along to get to the bottom of it.

Ten minutes, AO had said.

That gave me seven minutes to get to Food Mart.

I didn't know what the hell was happening, but was too afraid to not do what AO had told me and feel that torment again. Slipping on my jacket, I grabbed my keys from the bowl by the front door and left.

# THREE

The Food Mart always closed at seven on weekdays. There was one other car in the lot. It probably belonged to the guy who mopped and buffed the floors.

The lot's lights had been turned off. I looked around for a red Mustang in the dark.

Was I imagining this AO character the whole time?

No. I could see being a little fuzzy on things after I'd been laid off, but AO had messaged me hours before that.

Twin beams of light exploded in my rearview mirror, blinding me for a moment. Once my eyes adjusted, I left the Lumina to see what was behind me, nestled under the lone tree that grew in the lot.

Holding my hand up to shield my eyes, I felt a sickening dread wrap its meaty fingers around my chest.

It was a red Mustang.

Someone had to have turned on the lights. I ran to the door, anxious to see who this AO bastard was and why he was tormenting me. My instinct was to bash his teeth in. It would feel good to let some of the emotional air out. I realized I hadn't hit another man since college. I wasn't young or drunk this time, so maybe the outcome would be better than my foray into midnight beer muscles in Gary's Bar.

Shit, what if it was a woman? My nerves were so jangled, my anger riled up like a hornet, I wasn't sure I would be able to pull back my punch.

I grabbed the driver's door handle and yanked it open.

There was no one inside. New car smell washed over me.

"What the fuck?" I whispered, my words trailing off into the night air.

Looking back at my Lumina, I contemplated just going back home. A brief sparkler of pain singed the part of my brain that was behind my left eye. A rapid buildup of pressure made it feel as if it might pop out of its socket.

"Ow, ow, okay, I'll get in."

As soon as I sat behind the wheel and closed the door, the pain was gone. The relief was instant.

How was this possible? If it weren't for the periods of relief between flash-bursts of misery, I'd think I was having an extended delusion...or an aneurysm.

But aneurysms didn't make red Mustangs appear.

Unsure what to do next, I started up the car and waited. It didn't take long for the Bluetooth screen to alert me of an incoming text to voice. The tone was comfortingly feminine, but somehow I knew a man was behind the words.

"Right on time," it said. "Now, turn left on 302 and drive until you get to Wyndham. Once you cross the line, the online navigation system will take you the rest of the way."

"I'm not killing Marcellus," I muttered, putting the car in drive.

To my utter shock, the speakers blurted out, "Yes, you are! He ruined you and others today. People like him have come to the end of the line. You're going to make things right."

I just made the light, passing the gas station and heading east to the town of Wyndham.

"By killing a man?" I said. The car must have been bugged or something.

"By making things just."

"I've never killed anything before, other than some bugs and spiders. You picked the wrong pony for this." I didn't mention the pet newt I'd let starve to death, its body fusing to the rock, when I was ten. Death by neglect didn't constitute murder.

I drove past the drive-in, recalling how thrilled we'd been to go there for the first time when we moved up here. I hadn't seen a drive-in since I was a little kid. I'd thought there weren't any left. We'd been to it several times since. Katie loved being able to watch a movie outside in her little folding Disney princess chair. Candy and I had felt like kids ourselves.

As I crossed from Bridgton to Naples, I slammed on the brakes. There were no cars coming from either direction on the long stretch of road.

"I'm not doing this," I said. There was no way I was going to throw my life away just because some phantom lunatic was telling me to kill my boss. I'd lost my job. So had a ton of other people all across the country. We'd find a way to get through it. As long as I had Candy and Katie, nothing else mattered.

"You have to."

My eyes rolled in my head and I could no longer see the road. My brain was flooded with images of Marcellus. I watched him cook the books with our CFO, have multiple affairs, delight in the misery of others, abusing his power in his little fiefdom. I saw the monthly report his assistant provided, updating him with any negative news culled from social media on former employees. I could feel the thrill that ran through him when people he'd fired or had quit fell on hard times. Asshole. When the vision stopped, my heart was racing, and I couldn't control the swell of anger threatening to burst from my chest.

"That's why," the voice said from the speakers.

I floored the accelerator, blazing through the Naples Causeway, not giving a flying fart if there were any speed traps.

# THE FIRST ACT

# FOUR

Marcellus Hanson's house was a two-story ranch on steroids. It was nestled a quarter mile off the main road, a refuge of peace surrounded by nature. It had a three-car garage. There was a gazebo in the front yard.

*Bad quarter my ass*, I thought. This guy was living high on the hog while the rest of us struggled to make ends meet. Even in good years, our raises were barely in line with the cost of living standards.

*You won't have to worry about those crappy raises anymore.*

"I guess this is how you keep the bad stuff from coming to your home," I said inside the car. "Fuck everyone else over so you look like the hero and make your bonus."

I'd felt like a man possessed since the little freak show movie of Marcellus had spun through my cranium.

The lights were on downstairs. Marcellus's BMW was parked outside one of the closed garage doors.

"Look in the back seat," AO's female computerized voice said, startling me.

There was a long, black case on the floor. I reached around and placed it on my lap. Three clasps ran along one side of the case. I flipped each one open and looked inside.

"Holy..."

A long sword with a curved blade sat atop a blanket of black felt. It had a red leather handle. The craftsmanship was nothing short of divine. It must have cost a bundle.

"Do you like the scimitar?" the voice inquired.

"It looks like it could carve through brick," I said.

"It won't have to work quite that hard tonight."

Did the text-to-voice function just chuckle?

"He's about to leave his house. Get out of the car and cut off his head."

The scimitar was heavier than I thought it would be. A sliver of moonlight was snared by the blade's polished surface.

"I can't cut off a man's head," I said, feeling my rationality return.

An HD vision of Marcellus laughing when he made the decision to cut me loose rocked me. I could feel his satisfaction in getting rid of the Florida twerp.

Before I knew it, I was outside the car and striding to his porch.

Marcellus opened the door but didn't see me. I could smell his cologne from ten feet away.

*You arrogant dick. You're not going to use your flavor saver tonight.*

When he finally noticed me, I hid the scimitar behind my back.

"What the hell are you doing here?" he said, eyeing me like roadkill.

"I just wanted to talk," I said. "You never even gave me a chance to say a word in your office today."

"Look, what's done is done. If you don't leave, I'll call the cops."

"What if I beat the shit out of you before they get here?" The words stunned me. I'd never spoken like that before—not even in dreams!

He took a step back, closer to the safety of his door.

"I'm not kidding," he said, reaching for his cell phone. I ran up the wooden steps, brandishing the scimitar. His hand sliced away cleanly from his wrist, the cell phone still nestled in the palm.

The blade was so sharp, I didn't even feel any resistance as it cleaved through bone. The blood splatter was even kept to a minimum.

Marcellus cried like a deaf cat, clutching his arm.

"You sick fuck!" he wailed.

"Not me," I said. "I did everything right and played by the rules. You're the sick fuck, Marcellus. You lie and cheat and steal and think nothing will ever come back to bite you in the ass." I looked at his hand twitching on the porch. "Well, chomp, chomp!"

"Please, please, call an ambulance! I need help! Why are you doing this to me?"

"Because you earned it."

My hatred for the man swelled to an agonizing crescendo. There was only one way for this to go.

I brought the scimitar down into the center of his skull. It *thunked* all the way to his nose. One of his eyeballs rolled across the porch, flopping into an azalea bush. I pulled the scimitar free, flicking the blood off and onto his reddening shirt.

I heard his body hit the floor as I walked down the steps and back to the car. I put the scimitar in its case and started the Mustang. Every nerve and muscle in my body was humming as if I'd stuck a fork in an electrical outlet.

"Good work," AO said when I started the Mustang. "You can leave the car in the Food Mart lot and go back home. Candy and Katie will wake up several minutes after you've cleaned up and thrown your clothes in the fireplace."

"Huh?"

I looked down. My shirt and pants were dotted with flecks of blood.

Driving back to Bridgton felt like an out-of-body experience. I couldn't concentrate on the road. Luckily, it felt as if the Mustang was driving itself.

*You just killed a man. You didn't even give him a chance.*

I looked at my bloodshot eyes in the mirror.

"He didn't give me one either," I said, steering into the lot.

True to AO's word, after the fire had consumed the last of my shirt and pants, Candy and Katie awoke with twin yawns. It was almost eleven o'clock. The movie had stopped long ago, the menu playing on repeat.

"Wow, it's late," Candy said.

I went over to the couch, kissed the top of her head, and scooped Katie into my arms so I could carry her to bed. My legs were still a little shaky, but not so much that I'd drop my daughter.

"You were both really tired," I said.

*How can I act so damn normal after killing a man?* Despite my smile, I wanted to cry and bare my soul to Candy.

She turned the TV off and rearranged the pillows on the couch. "I'll meet you upstairs," she said.

"Daddy, are you sick?" Katie asked in her sleepy voice.

"No, honey. Why do you ask?"

The stairs creaked under my feet.

"You feel really hot, like when you have a fever."

She was back out before I slipped the sheet over her.

When I walked into the master bedroom, Candy was there, naked, waiting for me with a lustful look on her face that was usually reserved for special occasions.

"Take off your clothes and fuck me," she purred, parting her legs so I could see she had shaved herself bare earlier.

Despite everything that had transpired over the past six hours, I felt myself hardening.

"What got you so worked up?" I asked, lifting my shirt over my head. I climbed onto the bed, cupping her breasts, making her nipples stiffen.

"I think I need to take night naps more often," she said, pulling me in for a passionate kiss. "I don't wanna sleep, so you're going to have to keep me occupied."

Guiding my head down to her slick pussy, I forgot about everything.

# FIVE

When the alarm went off at six, I was tempted to throw it out the window. We'd just fallen asleep a few hours ago. My body was as sore as my mind was troubled. The sex had been amazing, momentarily erasing my firing and subsequent murder of my boss. At one point, when I'd entered her from behind, she'd gasped, "My god, your cock is so hard and hot. Just fill me and stay like that for a while."

I didn't even remember having sex this good on our honeymoon. For a few hours I was a stud, on top of the world, or at least, on top of my smoking hot wife.

With the light of a new day, my insides clenched as the gravity of my situation slammed me like a pouncing tiger. I kissed Candy and said, "You sleep in this morning. I'll get Katie ready for school."

She mumbled something into her pillow. I assume it was thanks.

I went downstairs to make Katie's lunch and packed it in her lunchbox. Getting her up and ready was a chore. My daughter is not a morning person.

There were tears, pleas for mercy, and a fit when I picked out the wrong outfit. How was I to know she wanted to wear her Dora shirt and not the Princess Jasmine top?

Her preschool was just a few blocks away. It was a mild morning, so I walked her instead of taking the car.

"How come you're not driving?" she said, her little hand in mine.

"I thought it would be a nice day for a walk."

"Are you going to walk all the way to work too?"

Her innocent remark reminded me of the conversation I'd have to have with Candy later. I squeezed her hand.

"I think I'll take the day off. That way, I can pick you up later. Maybe we can go to the park. Does that sound good?"

Her face lit up. "I love you, Daddy. Can we get pizza too?"

I longed to be her age again, when a trip to the park and a slice of pizza were all you needed to be happy.

"Sure."

As soon as she spotted her best friend Emma, she broke free from my grasp and went running with her into the school. I stood for a long time, just staring at the little building and wondering how on earth I was going to break the news to Candy. More importantly, should I tell her about Marcellus?

Candy was up when I returned and in her short robe that revealed the bottom curves of her bare ass when she lifted her arms above her head. She *did not* wear that robe when Katie was around.

"Taking a sick day?" she asked, filling a mug of coffee for me. "I wore you out pretty good, huh?"

A news commentator was talking about leaked information on Muslim jihadist sleeper cells in the Midwest and New England. Candy turned the radio off as she sashayed her way to me.

I felt sick to my stomach. I'd taken my box of belongings from my car and dropped it on the floor by the front door.

She wrapped her arms around me, nuzzling her head into my chest. "You haven't had a hooky day since we moved here. We could watch some movies and do a little you-know-what when the mood hits."

Taking a deep breath, I said, "We need to talk."

She stiffened. "Okay," she said, suspicion in her tone.

I told her that I'd been let go the day before. First she was angry for my not telling her last night, then freaked out wondering what would happen to us. I let her go through all the stages of unemployment grief. When her panic crested, she pulled me into her arms, consoling me.

"We'll be okay," she whispered in my ear. "We have savings. We can both get jobs. The pay up here isn't good, but we won't starve."

Would she feel the same way if she knew she was holding a cold-blooded murderer?

I was figuring out how to tell her what I did to Marcellus, dying inside at the thought of losing not just her but her love, when that heart-stopping pain returned. I went into a full body clench. She hugged me harder. "Don't worry, Peter. You've got me. Forever, no matter what."

She must have thought I was holding back tears, racked with grief.

How was she to know I couldn't confess my crime without having my brain explode?

Things settled down and we never got around to watching any movies. Nor did we do the other stuff she'd hinted at. But we did sit and talk and remember the early days of our marriage when we were broke enough to qualify for food stamps if we hadn't been too stubborn to apply for them. Instead, we existed on whatever pasta and tuna was on sale. At one point, I think I ate linguini with butter for ten days in a row.

Time flew by. I looked up at the kitchen clock and saw it was two.

"I promised Katie I'd pick her up," I said, searching for my sneakers. "I said I'd take her to the park and for a slice of pizza."

Candy grinned. "We're lucky to have you. Bring some pizza home for me. Let's take the weekend off from everything and just have fun. We can figure everything out later."

"I'd like that."

I gave her a long kiss and headed for the preschool. I got there just in time for the final bell. Cars and parents, mostly moms, were everywhere. I noticed one woman wearing a white surgical mask over her nose and mouth. She was either ill, or one of the lemmings who were easily led to panic by a media bent on instilling fear in a country already in the throes of 24/7 anxiety. I smiled her way but couldn't tell if she smiled back.

This was my first time picking Katie up from school. I was normally at work now, lost in budgets and ad copy. Two dozen kids spilled from the front door, four teachers (or were they helpers? I had no idea of the hierarchy in preschools) watching to make sure each child went with the correct parent.

Katie jumped into my arms. A heavyset woman with long, gray hair in a French braid said, "Is that your father, Katie?"

"Yes," she said. "He's taking me to the park!"

The woman gave me the once over, then nodded. "Have a nice weekend."

A man bumped into me as he tugged his son along. The little boy's mouth was pulled into a tight line. He did not look happy. Neither did who I assumed to be his dad. The portly man wore a well-practiced scowl as he towed his child into a waiting car, an old Nissan with faded paint and two crushed fenders.

"You want to walk to the park?" I asked.

"Okay," Katie said.

I could get to enjoy this. Time at home with Candy, getting fresh air, making Katie happy.

If I hadn't just killed a man, I might be able to savor these moments. Sure, Marcellus had been a monumental prick. From what I knew of him and saw in those weird visions, I didn't think he'd have a long line of mourners. But I had murdered him like I was some kind of maniacal vigilante. In the long run, was I any better than him?

Or was I worse?

It was only a five-minute walk to the park. I took a bench so I could watch Katie hit the slides.

My phone vibrated in my pocket.

There was a text from AO. I was tempted to toss the phone in the garbage. I wondered what the pain would be like if I did. Jesus, it took less than twenty-four hours to condition me like a lab rat. Was it weak of me to admit how soft I'd become? Did a double negative make a positive?

*Stop making jokes. There's nothing funny about this.*

Feeling my acid reflux kicking in, I opened the text.

**AO: That man u bumped into rapes his child.**

I looked around furtively, worried that another parent or child had seen what was on my phone.

*I wrote back: How can you know that?*

**AO: You're going to help his son tomorrow.**

I knew where this was headed. Everything got very dizzy, very fast.

**AO: The Mustang will be parked a block from your house. The man's address will be programmed. This one will be even easier.**

How could murdering another man be easier? I wanted to scream. My hands trembled too much for me to text back.

**AO: Trust me.**

I couldn't even trust myself anymore.

# JUSTIFIABLE

# SIX

It was kind of hard to enjoy a beautiful Saturday knowing that I was supposed to do something horrible to a total stranger. AO said the man outside the preschool raped his son. So, was I supposed to waltz up and give him the scimitar treatment based on the allegations in a text?

I was cracking up. I did my best to keep my distance from Candy and Katie, saying I had a headache and was nauseous.

"It's probably the stress," Candy said, offering me three Tylenol and a glass of water. "Go back to bed and take a nap. I'll take Katie to North Conway to play mini golf, give you some peace and quiet." She rubbed my arm, gently kissing the center of my forehead.

The television was on, tuned to CNN. The meteorologist dude looked absolutely giddy over the extreme weather patterns popping up all over the country and other parts of the world. Something about a shifting El Niño current, solar flares, and the same old rant about global warming.

Candy visibly shivered as she turned the TV off. "It's getting so I don't want to watch the news at all anymore."

"Thank you," I said, turning to my side. I could give a shit about a twister in Colorado at the moment.

As they left the house, my daughter shouted a hearty goodbye.

My phone was on the bedside table. I lay against my pillows, dreading the sound of an incoming text.

*Please, just leave me alone.*

There hadn't been anything on the local news about Marcellus. Now *that* I gave a shit about. I wondered how long it would be until someone found his rotting body on the porch. I also wondered how many critters were nibbling on him at this moment.

I barely made it to the bathroom, heaving up everything I'd eaten the day before. Searching the medicine cabinet, I found Candy's scrip for Xanax. She took it occasionally to sleep. She'd never recovered from Katie's almost yearlong bout of colic when she was born. All of her sleep mechanisms had been permanently damaged.

Taking two of the pills, I returned to the bed and squeezed my eyes shut, thinking of nothing until the pills took effect.

I awoke several hours later to the sound of a revving engine.

Bolting up in bed, I looked at my phone. It was dark and silent.

The big engine roared again.

My head swam a bit when I stood up. That Xanax was powerful stuff. It felt like my body needed another few hours to let it work itself out of my system. Shuffling to the window, the Xanax hangover was swept away in an instant.

The red Mustang purred in my driveway. The muscle car rumbled, smoke tailing from the exhaust.

"You motherfucker."

I ran down the stairs. This time, I'd catch that AO bastard. I darted to the driveway in my bare feet. The car was running. Just like two nights ago, I tugged the car door open. And just like the other night, there was no one inside.

"Get in," AO's feminine voice ordered through the car's speakers.

"Leave me the hell alone," I said, taking a step back.

That searing pain ripped through my skull. I think I cried out, staggering into the car. My chest slammed into the edge of the open door, adding to the pain.

Fire. Flames were everywhere, even when I opened my eyes this time. My house was a blazing inferno. So were all the homes on the block. Even the asphalt street was on fire, melting into a black pit of tar.

"No!" I clutched the sides of my head and jumped into the car to avoid the flames. As soon as my ass hit the seat, the pain was gone.

And so were the flames.

Everything had returned back to normal.

"Follow the navigation," AO said. "Hurry."

I closed the door and backed out of my driveway, hoping none of my neighbors saw me behind the wheel. I could just see Mrs. Robb next door coming up to Candy and saying, "When did you get the new sports car? Is that your husband's midlife crisis?"

"Please don't make me do this," I begged as I drove. The navigation system took me to the other side of

Bridgton. I hadn't done much exploring in this section yet. This was not the way I had envisioned seeing my adopted town.

As I drove down a road with a few houses in need of repair, AO said, "Stop right here."

I pulled onto the grass on the side of the road and hit the brakes.

"Take the case and walk around that bend. Look in the second window on the west side of the house."

"Then what?" I asked, grabbing the scimitar's case.

AO didn't respond.

I dropped the case on the back seat and crossed my arms.

The pain and fire came roaring back. It hit me so hard, like the waves in the Atlantic before a storm, that my forehead thumped off the steering wheel.

"Stop! I'll go!"

As soon as I touched the case, the agony abated.

I got out of the car and started walking. It was the middle of the afternoon. This was hardly the time or place to commit a crime. I knew I was going to get caught. I deserved to go to jail for what I did to Marcellus. I could face that.

But could I survive without Candy and Katie?

The shingles on the tiny, single-family home were a diseased gray. I figured they'd been slapped on the house sometime during Johnson's presidency. One of the windows had a hole in it, stuffed with a dirty rag. The roof was missing more tiles than I could count.

*People live in this?*

Bridgton was not a hick town by any means, but it did have a handful of what I called redneck pockets. All this house was missing was a ratty, mildew-infused sofa outside and an old clunker on cinder blocks. The house itself looked as if it were being consumed by the trees and wild vegetation that grew around it.

"Second window, west side," I huffed. I was a city boy. I couldn't tell west from north, even with a compass. I'd have to do some window peeking until I found whatever the hell it was I was supposed to be looking for.

The tall grass that sprouted alongside the house crackled as I prowled around, peering inside the dirty windows. These people had obviously never heard of Windex.

I saw an empty living room jammed with mismatched furniture, newspapers, empty cans of food, and an old tube TV. I didn't spot anyone, but I did hear noises coming from inside.

The next window gave me a glimpse of a small dining room. All it had was a table piled high with boxes and stacks of paper. Flower-print wallpaper was coming down in various places. What took me by surprise was the beautiful rosary that hung from the ceiling light fixture. It looked to be made of precious stones, each catching the light from the lone bulb.

I ducked away from the window when I heard a child crying. Circling to the other side of the house, I counted two windows and took a quick look.

What I saw got my molars grinding.

The man from the preschool was in the kitchen. I could see his fat, hairy ass. He wore a Red Sox jersey—Abreu—and stained socks.

But that wasn't what set fire to my core.

The little boy, his son, presumably, stood in front of the man, his head in direct line with the animal's genitals. I couldn't see what the boy was doing, but I didn't need to. I scrunched my eyes shut, willing the image away.

When I opened them, I was taken aback to see the scimitar in my hands. I had somehow removed it from its case without even knowing it.

The boy cried out. I looked back inside to see his father hit him on the side of his head.

"You can cry like a sissy when you're done," he grumbled, scratching at his dimpled ass.

The urge to slice him in half boiled within me.

"No," I said, gritting my teeth.

Not with the boy around. He couldn't be witness to it. But I couldn't stand around waiting for the abuse to end.

I found a brick in the grass. Eyeing an upstairs window, I heaved it as hard as I could. It blasted through the glass.

The man pulled away from the boy, tugging up his sweatpants.

"What was that?" the boy said, wiping his mouth with the back of his hand.

*Be calm, I thought. At least for another minute.*

"Stay right there!" the man yelled at him, dashing out of the room.

I ran to the back door, relieved to find it unlocked. The boy looked at me with resignation as if strange men coming into the house were a regular occurrence.

*And what were these strange men allowed to do with him when they came by?*

"Get out of here," I said to him. He was small for his age, with wide, brown eyes and unruly hair that curled down around his shoulders.

"Daddy said to stay," he said.

I showed him the scimitar. Fear swept the indifference from his eyes. "I said *go*!"

He tore out the door without looking back.

Great. He saw my face clear as day.

The man clumsily stomped around the floor above me.

I didn't care. It felt as if the scimitar was vibrating. Both it and I wanted to put it to good use.

Waiting at the bottom of the stairs, I listened to the man curse and holler out the window, threatening whoever had thrown the brick.

"You can stop your shouting," I called up the stairs.

The man's face popped into view as he leaned over the banister. He hadn't shaved in a few days and his teeth were a lovely shade of jaundice.

"Who the fuck are you?" he said warily. I kept the scimitar behind my back.

"The guy who threw the brick through your window," I said calmly, even though my heart was racing. It felt as if I had a fever brewing. Could a person get physically sick from watching such a heinous act?

"What the fuck you do that for?"

He took the first two steps down. I saw the slight bulge in the crotch of his sweatpants and had to hold myself back.

"To get your attention, you rapist pig," I said.

"What are you talking about?" He gave me a level look, playing it as cool as he could.

"I saw what you did."

"Oh yeah, what do you think you saw?"

"Not just a child, your own son." It was hard

keeping my voice even. "You're worse than a rutting pig, mister."

For the first time, I noticed the bat in his hand.

"You broke into my house. I have every right to kill you. The law's on my side," he said with a lopsided grin. "I could take you out right now and I'll get a fucking medal for defending myself and my property."

"I'm not a little boy you can scare. You want to kill me? Be my guest."

He gave a short laugh. "You're one dumb fuck."

Raising the bat over his head, he let out a phlegmy roar, charging down the stairs.

He swung the bat downward, hoping to crush my skull. The scimitar practically sang as it met the bat halfway through its arc, carving through the wood. The barrel clipped the man's shoulder before it fell to the floor.

"What the fuck?" he said, wide eyes staring at the severed bat.

"You need to expand your vocabulary," I said, ramming the handle of the scimitar into his considerable gut. The air whooshed out of him, along with a good deal of blood. He collapsed to the floor.

"No, no, please," he said.

I swung the scimitar, slicing the man's sweatpants open with the precision of a surgeon, exposing piss-stained tighty-whities.

"The cliché would be to cut off your cock and balls," I said.

He pushed himself along the floor with his heels, trembling hands held out in front of him.

"I didn't do anything," he said.

"Yes...you did," I said. "If you hadn't, I wouldn't be here."

I flicked the scimitar and several of his fingers bounced off the floor. Blood coated his shirt and face.

"Okay, okay, you're right. I'm sick. I can't help myself. My father did it to me. Please, just stop and I'll turn myself in." The disgusting turd wept and trembled. Tears ran down his grimy face as copiously as the blood that seeped from the open stumps where his fingers once resided.

I let the scimitar fall to my side.

"Get up," I said. "And start walking."

Pressing his good hand to the hole in his gut, he managed to get to his feet and headed for the front door.

"No, out back," I said.

He sobbed. "Why out back? Do you have a car parked there? I'll go with you to the police. But you gotta take care of my son."

As he stumbled outside, I said, "Your son would be better off alone in the woods in the dead of winter than with you."

"Wait, where's your car?"

With one quick swipe, I forged a horizontal crack in his ass. He fell to his knees.

The rage took full control. Before the man could drop another F bomb, I hacked away at him, pitting flesh and bone, exposing muscle and organs to the sun's afternoon rays.

When he started to scream, I sliced off his jaw. My brain burning, I brought the scimitar down on his collapsed body again and again, using the blade to douse the fire within me.

After God knows how long, I staggered back, mesmerized by the red mass of undistinguishable viscera steaming in the grass. There was no way to know the pile of gore had ever even been human. It looked like someone had dumped a bucket of chum in the yard.

All of my pent-up anger bled away. I was dizzy, shaky.

When the boy popped out from behind a tree, seeing what I'd done, I wanted to throw up.

Holding it together, I said, "Do you have any family nearby?"

His little head nodded. "My Aunt Mary lives over there." He pointed into the trees.

"You should go to her," I said, close to passing out.

He turned tail and ran as fast as a chipmunk.

I puked several times getting to my car, laying the blood-soaked scimitar back into its case.

*As I drove home, I kept thinking, The boy knows I killed his father. He'll tell the police. I puked up enough DNA for even a blind cop to find. I'll get the death penalty for murdering a child abusing scum.*

For the first time since our unholy union, AO remained silent during the drive.

# SEVEN

"Maybe I should take you to the doctor," Candy said, shaking down the thermometer.

I lay in bed, my head propped up by three pillows. My wife had stripped the comforter away as soon as she took my temperature.

"I don't feel bad enough to go crying to the doctor," I lied. The truth was, ever since I returned from mincing the child molester, I was racked with a headache, stomach cramps, and felt as weak as a newborn hamster. I'd parked that damned Mustang around the corner from my house and barely made it to my bed. Candy came home, saw the state I was in, and immediately went into nurse mode.

"Your fever is just over 103. If it goes any higher, I'm taking you no matter what you say. Anything over 104 can be dangerous, honey."

"I'll be fine," I said. My throat felt as if I had chugged a glass filled with tiny needles. "You gave me some Tylenol and a washcloth, now all I need is a nap."

Deep inside, a part of me was screaming. How

could I act so relatively normal in the face of what I'd done? I wanted to confess to Candy, but the words wouldn't come. Every time I wanted to even hint at the hideous acts I'd committed, the room would spin. In my silence, I kept reminding myself of the nature of the two men I had removed from the population. Maybe it wasn't as bad as I was making it out to be. Culling the herd wasn't necessarily a bad thing as long as wastes of life were the ones getting culled.

She washed my face with the cool, wet cloth.

"I'm keeping a close eye on you," she said. "I just hope it's not stress that weakened your immune system. Even when Katie's not sick, she's still a carrier from being around all those little snot noses in school."

Candy smiled and I so wanted to smile with her. The best I could do was pat her hand.

Katie must have heard her name, because she popped into the bedroom. "Hey, Daddy, you wanna see what I won at golf?"

She was carrying a business card. I did my best not to look like a terminal, murdering monster.

Taking the card, I said, "Wow, a free game. You really got a hole-in-one on the eighteenth hole?"

"Uh-huh."

I looked at Candy. She said, "She did it all by herself. I think we have a little Michelle Wie on our hands. Now, let's give Daddy some time to rest."

"Are you sick?" Katie asked.

"Just a little bit," I replied. Her tiny fingers caressed my cheek.

"I'll kiss you and make it allll better." Her lips touched my forehead.

"Thanks, baby. That's exactly what I needed."

Candy picked Katie up and said, "I'll be back to check on you later." She turned the TV on and lowered the sound. The moment they left the room, I was pulled, as if by some outside force, into a deep, troubled sleep.

When I awoke, it was dark outside. I couldn't recall any of my dreams, but I was filled with an oppressive foreboding.

"The sleep of the guilty," I mumbled, sitting up.

On the plus side, my head and stomach felt fine. The sheets were damp with my sweat. Physically, I felt good. I must have burned off whatever infection was trying to take hold.

Was that what this was—a killing virus? Take two pills and just sweat it out. Toss those soaking sheets, and AO, into the washing machine and carry on. It's not my fault. The virus made me do it.

Making my way downstairs, I saw Katie at the dining room table wearing headphones connected to the iPad. The screen was cracked but it still worked fine. I couldn't tell what she was watching, but it kept her engrossed enough not to notice me.

"Honey, should you even be up?" Candy said, rushing to me.

I smiled. "I'm okay. I told you, all I needed was a nap."

She felt my forehead. "I think it was my love and attention that did it."

"And Katie's kiss," I added.

Candy grabbed my hand and walked me to the living room. "I didn't want Katie to see or hear this."

Despite her vow to keep away, the news was on. There was a breaking story about a murder in Bridgton. A female reporter stood outside a ramshackle house. The sound was so low, I couldn't hear what she was saying—not that I needed her commentary.

Candy's grip on my hand tightened.

"They found the body of a man this afternoon. He's the father of one of the kids at Katie's school."

I thought I was going to pass out. I plopped onto the couch.

"Someone butchered him," she said. "I thought things like that didn't happen up here."

I could only shake my head. Cops and firemen flitted back and forth behind the reporter.

"What about the boy?" I asked, looking at the TV but replaying what I had done in my mind.

"He ran away," she said. "They say he watched as his father was killed. The poor kid. I don't know how a child can ever recover from something like that. I wonder if they'll cancel school on Monday. I'm just so sick about this, Peter."

She snuggled close to me. I put my arm around her.

Candy didn't question how I knew there'd been a boy in the house. She was too wrapped up in the horror of the story. I couldn't believe how stupid I'd been, opening my mouth before I thought.

The boy saw my face plain as day. He was probably describing me to the police right now.

As we watched, I wished for another fever to sweep me back out to the sea of nightmares. At least they weren't real.

# EIGHT

I faked sleep for as long as I could. Candy was a super light sleeper. I had to remain exceedingly still so as not to wake her. By four in the morning, I couldn't take it anymore. It felt like hissing cockroaches were scuttling under my skin. I had to get up.

Candy didn't stir as I crept out of the room. I checked in on Katie. She'd kicked her covers off and was clutching her Build-A-Bear purple pony.

Sitting at the kitchen table, I went online to see if there'd been any developments in the story. I also wanted to see if anyone had discovered Marcellus's body yet. If not, odds were high that it had been dragged off by some of the local wildlife, left to molder in the woods. He'd be declared a missing person before a corpse.

I checked *The Portland Press Herald*, saw the front page crammed with stories on the weather and the strange virus that had hit several major cities. Were the people who had the virus getting strange messages and killing bad people too?

No, they were just sick, plain and simple. Sick and dying, not sick and murderous. News like this would have raised my blood pressure considerably, but I had something else on my mind.

It wasn't until page five when I saw an article about the man I'd killed yesterday. It said there was a sketch of the murderer on page two.

*Oh god, this is where my life ends.*

My finger swiped to the next page. What I saw nearly made me fall off my chair.

The man in the sketch wasn't me at all!

A burly Hispanic man wearing a baseball cap glowered at me. He had a small scar under his right eye.

How the hell had the kid come up with that? I was a skinny White guy with a well-kept beard. That man couldn't be more opposite me.

And the more I looked at him, the more familiar he became to me.

My hand flew to my mouth.

I'd seen that man before. He worked in the produce section at the supermarket. He'd once opened a new box of Bartlett pears for me to make sure I got the freshest ones.

What the fuck was going on here?

On the one hand, I was relieved that my door wasn't in danger of being broken down by the police. On the other, heavier hand, I was a two-time murderer and now an innocent man was getting framed for one of my crimes.

Pushing back from the table so hard I almost knocked my chair down, I stormed into the living room and found my phone. I went back to the kitchen.

"Where the hell are you now, AO?" I hissed, checking for new texts.

I not only didn't find new texts—all of AO's previous texts were gone. Wiped clean, as if they'd never happened. The same with my email account.

I ran to the sink to throw up.

"What if I've been imagining everything?" I said between hot gouts of bile.

I cleaned up fast, grabbed my coat, and left the house. The streetlights were still on and there were no signs of the sun coming up any time soon. Good. I didn't exactly want my neighbors to see me traipsing around the streets in my pajamas with flecks of vomit on my mouth.

The Mustang was gone too. A new, white Honda was parked in the space where I'd left it. Collapsing on the sidewalk, I pressed my face into my palms.

Losing my job had caused a psychotic break. I'd been normal up to that point. Maybe the messages I'd received before I went into Marcellus's office was just a convenient lie I'd told myself so I wouldn't think what I was thinking now.

And despite my insanity, I'd committed two crimes and gotten away with them.

"I have to turn myself in."

My ass was soaked from sitting in the morning dew.

First, I had to tell Candy. She had to know why I was going to the police station, why I had to distance myself from her and Katie.

If I had convinced myself that someone called AO made me kill those two men, it wasn't safe for me to be around my own family.

Katie slept past six a.m. for the first time I could ever remember. That meant Candy was also asleep. I paced around downstairs, watching the local news, feeling parts of my soul dissipate with every report of the murder.

Finally, just after eight, I heard my daughter's light footsteps tip-tap into my bedroom, followed by the sound of Candy laughing.

They'd come down in a couple of minutes. I'd have to fake being normal for Katie and find a way to get Candy alone. My heart's rhythm went so out of whack, I found it hard to breathe, my lungs hitching like a world-class stutterer.

"Daddy!" Katie yelped when she saw me, her pony in tow. I kneeled down so I could catch her as she threw herself at me.

"Good morning, lazy bones," I said. "You slept late today."

"I did?"

I kissed her cheeks and the tip of her nose. "You sure did. You must have been having some real nice dreams."

She arched an eyebrow. "I don't know," she said, shrugging her shoulders. "I can't remember."

"You want some cereal?"

She nodded.

"Okay, take a seat in the kitchen and I'll get it for you."

I thought my knees were going to give out on me a couple of times as we walked hand in hand. I found her favorite cereal, nearly dropping the bowl as I took it from the cabinet.

"Morning, honey," Candy said, dressed in her mommy robe and fuzzy slippers.

Plopping Katie's cereal in front of her, I said to Candy, "I need to talk to you in the living room."

She looked concerned. I didn't have a good poker face.

"Sure. Katie, baby, we'll be right back."

"Okay, Mommy."

Candy slipped her hands in mine. "What's up, Peter? You look like you're having a panic attack."

"I have something to tell you and I need you to stay calm," I said. I swallowed hard, fighting back another bout of nausea.

She said, "I know this is hard for you and even when I tell you we're going to be all right, it doesn't feel like it at the moment. I'm glad you're talking to me. Tell me whatever you're feeling so we can work through it together."

I looked into her hazel eyes and saw so much love there. Would that love remain when I confessed? I didn't want to lose her. It would be easier if I just shut up.

No! When I'd taken those lives, I'd already lost her by destroying myself.

"Candy, look, I...I..."

The tempest of pain came roaring back, shattering my skull like it has been carpet bombed. I strangled out some kind of cry and felt my bowels let loose, shitting myself with such force, I thought I'd ruptured something. I felt Candy's hand on me but couldn't hear her.

Before I blacked out, I saw the fire again, a hundred-foot-high wall of flame, consuming everything in its path. Candy and Katie reached out for me within the flames, pleading for help, their flesh turning black, cracking and popping until they collapsed out of sight.

# MADNESS

# NINE

This time, I woke up in a curtained-off section of Bridgton Hospital's emergency room. There was an IV in my arm and a cannula under my nose. Candy jumped from the chair beside my bed and brushed the hair from my forehead.

"Oh, thank God," she said. "I was so worried."

My head was groggy. There must have been some kind of sedative in the IV.

"What happened?" I said.

"You had a seizure. I called the ambulance. You were still seizing when they got you here. When it stopped, you passed out."

I tried to lift my head from the pillow. That wasn't happening.

"What time is it?" I asked.

She checked her watch. "Almost ten."

"At least I wasn't out long," I said, attempting to muster a smile.

"It's ten at night," she said.

"I've been unconscious for over twelve hours?"

"Yes."

"Where's Katie?"

"She's with Huey and Anne next door. I just checked on her half an hour ago. She's asleep on their couch."

"Did...did she see what happened?"

Candy's eyes shimmered. "She did. She was scared, but I was able to calm her down. When I told her you were all right, she said she was going to make you some get well soon cards."

I felt like I was made of oatmeal. I didn't think I had the strength to lift a soda can.

"Did the doctors say what happened?"

"They think you have a viral infection," Candy said. "You were burning up when you got here, just like yesterday."

"Did they take a CAT scan or anything?"

I thought maybe I had a brain infection or a tumor. That would explain the whole AO delusion and my violent behavior. There was a glimmer of hope that even when I told the cops what I did, I could still be free if I was a victim of a debilitating illness. I could have my life back, if the illness didn't kill me. It was disheartening to realize that this was my best case scenario.

"I don't know. They've been taking you in and out for all kinds of tests. I'm going to get a nurse and let her know you're up."

Candy pulled the curtain aside. I could see a corner of the nurse's station. The loudspeaker beeped, and a female voice called out for a Dr. Fass.

My wife disappeared from view. I felt as if I were melting into the hospital bed. I had only been awake for a few minutes and already I wanted to go back to sleep.

My eyes were just starting to close when I heard a door slam open, followed by hurried footsteps and a lot of urgent chatter.

"We have a code blue!" a man shouted.

I heard a stretcher being wheeled next to me, but I couldn't see what was going on because of the curtain. Controlled bedlam was the best way to describe it. Doctors and nurses rushed into the space, making the curtain billow in and out. The person next to me was in a bad way. Recalling my days of watching *ER* on TV, I was pretty sure code blue meant the person next to me had stopped breathing.

"Heparin, now!" a doctor ordered.

Machines were plugged in, beeping to chaotic life.

"Who is he?" I heard a nurse ask someone just outside where I lay.

"The guy who they say murdered that man behind his house," a male voice said.

My own heart seized.

The man continued, "He was attacked by a relative of the man outside the gas station. Stabbed him with a butcher knife. He coded the moment we got him in the truck."

Where was Candy? I needed her with me, to hold my hand, to tether me to the dwindling parts of my life that were sane.

A woman shouted, "Where's my Eddie?"

"Miss, I need you to stay right there. The doctors are working on your husband right now."

"I want to see him!"

"Clear!" someone blurted next to me. There was a

high-pitched whine. I didn't need to see to know what was happening.

"Oh my god, is he in there?"

"Please, come with me. We have to let the doctors do their job."

"Eddie!"

A fresh wave of voices swept into the emergency room. What the hell was going on? Candy rushed back to my side.

"What's happening?" I asked.

"I don't know. It's crazy. They brought a man in with a knife sticking out of his stomach. That's his wife outside. I snuck past the nurses when a bunch of guys came in. They look mad as hell."

"Where the hell is security?" a woman cried out.

This was Bridgton. I doubted very much they had much call for more than one security guard. Only hospitals in big cities would have the personnel to quell this madness.

"You!" the dying man's wife shrieked.

"I came to see if Eddie was all right," a man said.

"So you can gloat to your brother that he killed my husband?"

Candy grabbed my hand. I wished to hell I could see through the curtain, but on the other hand, I hoped it was enough to shield us from the escalating insanity.

"You goddamn son of a bitch! You took my husband from me! Aaaiiieeeee!"

Something crashed to the floor and a rugby scrum erupted outside the curtains. A man yelped in pain. The woman screamed that someone had stabbed her.

I lifted myself off the pillows, gripping Candy's

hand. If the fight spilled into here, there was nothing I could do to defend her.

Everyone was shouting, bodies smashing into walls. A man with long hair and glasses collapsed. From under the curtain, I saw blood oozing from his ear. Candy scrambled back as far as she could go without releasing her hold on me. The man's eyes rolled up in his head. A white hospital shoe stepped on his face as a nurse ran away.

Suddenly, a gun went off, bringing a merciful silence to the riot.

# TEN

When the dust finally settled, the case of mistaken identity was responsible for three deaths, including the man who'd been brought in with the knife in his stomach (the doctors were too busy saving themselves to save him) and four wounded. By the time Candy and I were allowed to leave our little curtained-off corner, a porter was mopping blood off the white tiled floor. There were more police than medical staff in the emergency room. I saw several state troopers and even cops from nearby towns. All of their faces were drawn and pale, unaccustomed to scenes of such brutality, in a place of healing, no less.

I was released from the hospital the next afternoon, only after the police had shut down the hospital and questioned all who were in the emergency room when the fracas broke out. I wondered where the truly sick and wounded were taken during those hours. For all I knew, the nearest hospital was fifty miles away—or in the next town over.

Candy and I were questioned for a bit. The doctors wanted to make sure I was all right to go home.

I knew I didn't have a viral infection, just like I knew I was responsible for the collapsing dominoes of death that followed my actions. Tension was high in the town when we stopped at the variety store to pick up some cans of Katie's favorite iced tea. Folks were talking. Half were afraid, and the other half were quietly calling for even more justice. It didn't take a genius to fathom that their idea of justice skirted the traditional involvement of police and the court system.

Is this all it took to strip the civility from a quiet little town? My head spun the whole car ride home, but I didn't let on to my wife.

Candy set me up in bed before getting Katie from our neighbors. Deep lines of worry etched across her forehead and the corners of her eyes.

"I don't think I'll ever get the sound of everyone screaming out of my head," she said.

"Why don't you lie next to me for a bit before getting Katie? You look like you're going to collapse."

"No, I'll feel better with her home. Maybe we'll all lie down and fall asleep to some boring daytime TV."

I rolled onto my side when she left, staring out the window.

What had I done? If I confessed now, I'd probably get the death penalty.

But then, maybe that's exactly what I deserved.

The sound of my phone vibrating on my night table froze my blood. I was too terrified to pick it up. I pulled the covers over my head, muffling its cries to be held. A tiny pinpoint of heat emanated from between my eyes.

"Oh no," I muttered, tensing further with dread.

The phone kept vibrating. I pictured it dancing off the table and shattering on the floor.

The heat seeped into my closed eyes. It got to the point where I thought for sure they were going to melt, just like the pale slugs in my parents' yard used to sizzle away when we poured salt on them. Lashing out, I grabbed the phone while pushing the sheets away from my face.

My hand trembled. My thumb was barely able to swipe the text icon.

**AO: You have nothing to feel guilty about.**

"I've lost my mind," I said, holding the phone with two hands so it didn't drop. "This can't be happening."

**AO: You're not, and it is. This is only the beginning.**

"Get the fuck out of my head!"

**AO: You may rest today. The Mustang will be waiting for you tomorrow. You'll drive to Saco in the afternoon.**

I no longer saw the need to text. Why bother when the great and mysterious AO could read my mind? It was all the proof I needed that I'd gone irretrievably insane.

"And if I say no?" I asked, knowing the answer.

**AO: You won't. Here's why.**

My body went stiff as a board as a hurricane of images shot through me like a ballistic missile. I saw a school, a blur of kids streaming past me. I couldn't tell their ages. Something exploded behind me. The hallway turned red as hundreds of voices screamed.

I felt something tear through my stomach and I jolted from the vision with a burst of pent-up air.

On the verge of hyperventilating, I stared at the phone still clutched in my hand.

"I am not going to a school to murder children. You can kill me with that pain you put in my head, damn you! I won't do it."

I realized that if Candy was home, she could hear me. Maybe it was for the best if she did and called psychiatric services to fetch me.

**AO: Trust in me.**

"Trust in you? Because of you and what you've made me do, people are dead. Lives are ruined."

**AO: Or saved. It depends on your perspective.**

I thought of the nurse who'd accidentally been shot at the hospital. How did she fit in to all of this? Did she deserve to die? Had anyone who had lost their lives over the past few days? Marcellus was an asshole, but the last time I checked, being an asshole wasn't a capital offense. The man who raped his son was a monster, but like Frankenstein's monster, was he to blame for being what nature had made him to be? Sure, he should have been in prison, maybe even for life, but dead?

"Where are you?" I looked at the closed closet doors opposite the bed, picturing some golem-like creature, AO made physical, leering at me through the slats, plotting the next move to keep me under its control.

**AO: Sleep now. Tomorrow, you'll see.**

Before I could protest, everything went black.

# DEEPER

# ELEVEN

To my surprise, I woke up the next morning feeling refreshed and full of energy. Candy was already down-stairs with Katie. I heard the microwave pinging, alerting Katie that breakfast was served.

I looked at my phone. There were no messages from AO. In fact, there was no record of AO's texts to me the previous day—or any day for that matter. The sweet smell of cinnamon oatmeal wafted up the stairs.

*I'm supposed to go to Saco*, I thought while I peed. AO's urging to trust him seemed just as ludicrous after a good night's sleep.

So why wasn't I contemplating how to get out of my next mission? Would my cell phone self-destruct in ten seconds? No, AO needed it to reach me. Yeah, sure, it was the phone that made me do it!

"I hope you don't mind that I kept Katie home," Candy said, holding a mug of steaming coffee between both hands. "With everything that's happened, I think it's best she stays home for a while. I'll feel better."

I kissed the top of her head. "I totally agree. It's not

like she's missing anything crucial in preschool anyway. If we keep her home for the week, she may fall behind in her finger painting skills, but I can live with that."

Candy exhaled with a bright smile. "I don't know why I was so worried you'd be upset. How do you feel?" She felt my forehead with the back of her hand.

"Fine. I'm just happy to be out of the hospital"

"They said on the news today that there were four separate assaults in town last night. It's like the whole place has gone crazy."

"All the more reason to stay inside with Katie today. I'm going to take a ride to Portland, see if I can catch up with Jimmy V. Maybe he has an opening, or knows someone who does."

I knew Jimmy Valentine from when we worked at a credit and collections company, my first job out of college. Jimmy had moved to Maine several years ago and opened up his own consulting business.

Not that I had any intention of seeing him. The trip to Portland and back was roughly the same as Saco, about two hours. I needed a good excuse to be out of the house for a while.

"That's a great idea! It's always who you know," Candy said. "Now, you sit while I make you some oatmeal."

I said good morning to Katie, but she was so engrossed by SpongeBob SquarePants, she didn't even know I was there.

It seemed as if the Lumina drove itself to the old elementary school's parking lot on Depot Street. Auto pilot was becoming a common occurrence in my life. I wasn't surprised when I saw the red Mustang, parked close to the empty building.

First, AO could talk to me without my needing to text. Now I could find the muscle car without being told where it had been parked. All the more reason to believe this was some self-induced delusion. Did I have a split personality? What did I call myself when I bought the Mustang and the scimitar? Or did I just steal them? That seemed more in line with this new side of me.

I swapped cars. The case with the scimitar lay across the entire back seat. For the first time, I noticed the odd smell in the car—a hinting scent of foreign spices. I looked for an air freshener but could find none.

AO didn't make an appearance during the drive to Saco. The radio didn't work, even though the car looked brand new, so I drove in silence.

It wasn't until I passed the WELCOME TO SACO sign that AO spoke.

We had taken Katie to the water park in Saco when we first moved to Maine and I was lost in the memory of one of the best days of the summer. AO's simulated voice almost made me careen into the divider.

"The GPS system will take you the rest of the way," AO said.

"It better not lead me to a school," I said.

"It won't."

I passed an old factory building with the Saco River to my left. The GPS took me down winding residential streets. The neighborhood went from upper middle class to don't-keep-your-doors-unlocked in just several blocks. Here, the weather-beaten Cape houses were caged in by rusted, twisted chain-link fences. There were more "Beware of Dog" signs than I could count. A startling number of angry pitbulls eyed me as I passed.

"You have arrived," the GPS chirped cheerily as I stopped in front of a two-story, two-family house. The front steps were missing a board and the screen door was off its hinges, leaning against one of the windows.

"Do I take the scimitar?" I asked, worried that if I didn't, that damned agony would return.

"Of course," AO said. "The door is open. Go inside quietly. When you get to the bedroom at the back of the house, you will have truly arrived at your destination."

I looked to see if anyone was around. The neighborhood was empty, save for a few barking dogs. That didn't mean people weren't watching the flashy sports car from behind thin curtains or slatted blinds.

Carrying the case under my arm, I slowly opened the door, careful not to shout, "Is anyone home?" I sensed AO wouldn't have appreciated that. The smell of yesterday's dinner and dust enveloped my head. The inside of the house was surprisingly neat, though the furniture was worn and threadbare. There was a big, new, flat-screen TV in the living room. In the kitchen, dishes had been left to soak and the table for four was littered with crumbs.

*And that's how you get ants.*

I almost laughed out loud.

What the hell was happening to me? I just broke into a home carrying an Arabic sword days after murdering two people, and all I could think of were funny one-liners.

Screw stealth. I was crazy. I needed to be caught. If I tried to turn myself in, the power I had given to this fantasy AO would cripple me. So, what was to stop me from being discovered and taken in by the cops? It was better than having another death on my hands.

I *accidentally* caught my foot on a chair, spinning it into the wall.

"Who's there?" a voice, a boy's, cried out.

*Run, kid, run!*

I tromped to the back bedroom as instructed, making enough noise to rattle some of the pictures on the wall. I kicked the door in. A teenage boy jumped from his chair, eyes wide with shock.

The gun he held in his hand was massive. I was pretty sure it was the rock to my scimitar's scissors.

"Who the fuck are you?" the kid spat. I noticed how the gun didn't so much as quiver. He knew how to handle it and didn't seem hesitant to put a hole through me.

He was sixteen, maybe seventeen, with a shaved head—a tattoo of a dragon emblazoning one side. He wore a black Misfits sweatshirt, the white skeleton glaring at me, and black jeans.

I felt a burning need to piss myself. What the hell had I stumbled into?

"I said, who the fuck are you?"

That was a damn good question. If I said, "*I'm the guy my phone sent to kill you,*" I was pretty sure I'd be dead before I finished the sentence. The kid had eyes so dark, they bordered on black. I didn't detect an ounce of mercy in them.

It was then that I also noticed the array of firearms laid out on his unmade bed. There were pistols, a shotgun, grenades, boxes of ammunition, and several of what looked to be homemade pipe bombs.

In that instant, I realized what the vision of the school had meant. This jackbooted kid was planning to destroy his school. He had enough on that bed to kill a hell of a lot of kids.

A calming wave swept over me.

"You planning for a one-way trip?" I asked.

The kid cocked the hammer back on his gun. "What did you say?"

"When you're done," I said, nodding at the bed. "You going to off yourself, shoot it out with the police, or turn yourself in? Suicide seems to be the exit of choice for you kids. Which makes sense. I mean, once you do what you're planning to do, the fate of your afterlife is sealed. You're already going to burn in hell for eternity. Why spend the life you have left being punished as well?"

"I don't know what you're talking about."

"I think you do. If you shoot me now, your neighbors will hear. This place will be crawling with cops. Why don't you put the gun down?"

The air between us was sliced with a high-pitched bang.

It felt as if my leg had been kicked by a mule. I fell to a knee, watching blood seep from the tiny hole in my thigh.

The kid smiled. "That's why I have a silencer."

# TWELVE

What the hell had just happened? AO, or my demented mind, had sent me to a gunfight with a knife. Now, not only was Candy going to be a widow, but dozens of parents were going to lose their children. What was the sense of my coming here?

"To answer your question," the kid said, standing over me, the gun pointed at my face. "I'm smarter than all those other school shooters. I'm actually going to get away and live a new life in South America. I have it all mapped out."

He grinned, and in that moment, I knew I had seen pure evil for the first time in my life.

"I wasn't coming back here anyway, so I don't mind making a mess."

I feebly put my hands in front of my face as if they were made of Kevlar. From between my fingers, I saw him pull the trigger.

Nothing happened.

He pulled it again and again. The gun was jammed.

I rolled away from him, opening the latches on the scimitar's case.

"Hey!" he shouted as if to get me to stop so he could have an easy shot once the gun was working properly.

The scimitar nearly jumped into my hand. I lashed out without looking, feeling slight resistance. The kid looked down at his legs, his mouth in a frozen O. The blade had sliced through his shinbones as if they were made of cream cheese. Well, raspberry cream cheese.

The gun fell from his hand, finally going off. The bullet buried into the kid's side as he fell back onto the bed.

Getting to my feet, I rammed the blade down on his wrists, severing both hands and just missing one of the grenades.

"Oh my god!" the kid wailed. Gouts of blood pumped from the stumps, bathing him in gore.

"Too late to switch sides," I said.

I rammed the curved tip of the blade into his throat. It went through him and halfway into the mattress. His eyes bulged and more crimson bubbled from his mouth. Arterial spray painted the wall to my right. The kid's legs and arms spasmed for a bit, then went still.

The moment the light went from his eyes, the searing agony of the gunshot wound in my leg screamed for attention. In between my angry hisses of pain, I heard a door open and close.

Was this nightmare ever going to end?

"Ralph?" a woman's voice called out. "I just got a call from school that you cut class again. You better have a damn good excuse."

A middle-aged woman dressed in a Lady Gaga T-shirt, tight jeans, and high heels stopped in the bedroom's doorway. She had dyed blond hair and too much makeup. She looked every bit the part of the dried-up woman desperately wanting to be a MILF. Stale alcohol oozed from her pores.

"What did you do to my son? Aaahhhhhh!"

I pointed the bloody scimitar at her.

"You raised this monster?" I said, gritting my teeth from the pain in my leg and the anger at a parent that could allow a child to fall so far.

"I'm calling the cops! You murdered my boy!" She started backpedaling, hands fluttering around her mouth.

"I did the world a favor," I said.

As she turned to run, I cleaved her left shoulder with the scimitar. It took the breath right out of her. She fell face-first onto the floor, quickly flipping over so she could beg for her life.

"Please, I didn't do anything to you," she said, all concern for her son gone now that she was facing her own mortality. "If you leave me, I won't tell the cops that I saw you. I'll tell them I came home and found Ralph dead."

Her plea made me physically ill because I knew she would be true to her word. She cared more about herself than her child.

"Don't bother," I said, swinging the scimitar like a pendulum. Her head rolled away from her body, settling against the baseboard. Her eyes blinked hard several times. I had to stop myself from kicking her right between them.

# THIRTEEN

I limped out of the house, pausing on the porch steps to see if anyone was about. That woman had a loud voice. Someone must have heard her.

The streets were empty. Even the dogs had stopped barking.

"Ah, Jesus," I cried, clomping down the stairs. My thigh both burned and felt as if live wires had been run through the savaged meat. The scimitar's case kept me unbalanced. It was a chore getting into the car. I tossed the case into the passenger seat. The Mustang started up on its own. I backed out of the driveway, laying down rubber as I sped away from the house. So much for a quiet exit.

"Come on, talk to me, AO," I shouted, taking a turn a little too fast and almost sideswiping a line of parked cars. I had to get the hell out of Saco.

If AO was a figment of my imagination, the muscle car was all too real. As I rocketed onto the highway's ramp, I wondered where I had gotten the car. Had I stolen it? Or had I owned it all this time, the *sane* side of me never realizing what the *insane* side had in store.

The bullet wound was just as real. My jeans were wet with blood. Did it sever an artery? I was too sick with worry to look. I had to see a doctor, but if I did, they'd have to call the cops once they realized I had a bullet buried in my leg. I was good and fucked. If I chose to ignore it, hope the bullet had gone all the way through and a tight bandage and some antibiotics were all I needed, how could I get in the house without Candy noticing?

I had to settle down. I moved the Mustang into the center lane. Even though I was going seventy in a sixty-five-mile-an-hour zone, a steady stream of cars flew past me on either side.

"What now?" I asked, hands locked at ten and two. My right foot squished when I pressed down on the pedal, my blood saturating the sock. "You're leaving me hanging out to dry?"

A pickup flashed its brights behind me. It rode my ass so close, I could see the color of the driver's eyes—Sinatra blue. The guy had long hair and a week's worth of carefully sculpted stubble. Metrosexual meets modern day metal head.

"Go around me, asshole." I waved him to get in the fast lane and leave me be.

If I didn't go to a hospital, I could call ahead to Candy and tell her to meet me at the diner for lunch. That would get her out of the house so I could get the first-aid kit and a fresh pair of jeans. But how would I explain the limp? I shook my head. Coming up with a lie on how I hurt my leg was the least of my problems. I'd call home once I got a little closer. She wouldn't recognize me if we passed on the road. In that sense, the Mustang was good camouflage.

A horn blared behind me, an unbroken stream of impatience and stupidity.

"Are you fucking kidding me?" I said, staring into the rearview mirror. The guy was glowering back at me. The circus of cars had broken. He had the entire damn road to go around me. Just pick a lane.

I slowed the car down. If he was in such a hurry, he'd figure it out.

Gritting my teeth, I chanced poking a finger around the bullet hole in my thigh. I winced, but more from expecting thunderbolts of pain rather than actually feeling anything. The pad of my index finger came away sticky with blood. I touched it again, wondering how deep the wound went. I was probably making any potential infection worse by prodding it with my dirty finger, but so what.

To my shock, I touched solid, unblemished skin.

"What?"

I looked down, pulling the hole in my jeans up so I could see the flesh underneath.

*Hooooooonnnnnnkkkkk!*

"Holy mother of—how the hell?"

The hole had been there, as evidenced by the pain and copious amount of blood on my pants and the car.

But now it was gone. I wiped the blood away and saw my unblemished thigh, the hair tinted crimson.

*Hoooooooonnnnnnnkkkk!*

I looked up. The pickup was inches away from my trunk. Was this guy insane?

Elated and pissed off that this jackhole was spoiling the moment, I slammed on the brakes, not thinking about the fact that the pickup was going to plow right through me. The truck rammed into the rear of the Mustang. My car was rocketed into overdrive. I slammed back into my seat, my hands trying to keep the wheel straight.

Suddenly, the pressure from behind was gone. The back of the Mustang fishtailed.

"Where the hell—"

I jumped in my seat when the pickup dropped in front of me, landing on its roof. The truck was still going over sixty miles an hour, kicking up a fireworks display of sparks.

Cutting the wheel to my right, I swerved around the truck, nicking one of its fenders, sending it spinning. I watched in my rearview as the truck whirled off the road, coming to a great, heaving stop at the base of a thick-trunked tree. All that was missing was a theatrical fireball.

I kept on going. A strange heat flushed my skin. My balls felt as if they were on fire.

I felt good.

Holy shit, I felt more than good. I felt amazing.

Somehow, I knew the man in the pickup was dead. Knowing that gave me a strange sense of...accomplishment.

In under an hour, I'd killed three people, and I never felt so alive.

My hands burned so hot I thought the steering wheel would melt in my palms. My vision wavered between blurred edges and the clarity to see all the way into Canada.

What the hell was happening to me?

Instead of my usual Cobb salad, I dove into a double cheeseburger deluxe at the diner, sucking down a large Coke and a chocolate milkshake. The last time I'd been this hungry was back in high school when I was on the track team, carbo-loading for a race. Katie nibbled on my fries and took sips from my shake.

"I did feed you breakfast," Candy said, staring at my plate.

"My meeting with Jimmy V didn't go so well. I guess I'm a nervous eater."

"You never were before."

"I never really had much to be nervous about I guess."

The truth was, for the first time in my life, there wasn't a nervous cell in my body. When I changed clothes back home, the throbbing heat had bled from my body, but I was still hyper-charged.

Because of all the unrest in the town, we were the only people in the diner. Candy was uneasy, but I was hungry.

"Mommy, I'm tired," Katie said, leaning her head back against the vinyl booth.

I was just sucking up the dregs of my milkshake. "Okay, let's get you home for a nap," I said, tucking thirty bucks under the saltshaker.

The drive down Main Street was eerie. It was the middle of the day and there wasn't a soul on the streets. I noticed that even half the stores were closed. People were scared. Others angry. And still others, grieving.

Candy put Katie to bed while I went to the kitchen looking for cookies.

"I will not endure a fat, unemployed husband," my beautiful wife said when she walked into the kitchen.

"One day of being a pig will not make me fat. Besides, I think I lost my appetite...for food."

I slipped my arm around her waist and pulled her to me. We kissed, long and hard. "You should have more bad meetings," she said, rubbing my cock outside my jeans. I undid her bra and pulled her shirt over her head, sucking her thick nipples. My hand felt the heat of her sex, caressing her.

The buttons of her jeans popped off, clattering on the linoleum floor. I tugged her pants off and lay her on the kitchen table.

She held my head for a moment and said, "What if Katie wakes up?"

"Then we'll have gotten the whole 'getting caught by our child' trauma out of the way."

Before she could offer a counterargument, I wrapped my mouth around her pussy, pushing my tongue inside her. She moaned, locking my head between her thighs. Slickening two fingers in her yearning muff, I gently inserted them in her ass. She nearly bucked off the table. Candy came in my mouth. I greedily drank her in.

Her cheeks bloomed as she pushed herself from the table. "Your turn," she said with a wicked smile.

I jumped out of my jeans, briefly looking down at my thigh to make sure it was still all right. It was then I noticed my flaccid cock. How was that possible? Just thinking of sex with Candy got me rock hard—every time.

"Hope you didn't wear yourself out after that big

meal," Candy said, caressing it in her hand. "I know how to wake him up."

She took it in her mouth, all the way to my balls, which she cupped with one hand. The vibration of her moaning on my member should have been enough to send me skyrocketing.

But the more she did, the softer I became.

"Honey, I don't know why, but—"

"We can try again later," Candy said. "You're under a lot of stress. It's totally understandable."

I smiled down at her, but I felt like screaming. This didn't happen to me! How could I feel so alive and be so dead down there? It didn't make any sense. Candy's silky, naked curves were inviting me to explore every inch and I couldn't even grow a damn centimeter.

"What's more important is that I made you feel good," I said, attempting to recover any sense of manhood I had left.

She rubbed her inner thigh. "That you did. Wow."

We dressed, somewhat awkwardly, and settled onto the couch, falling asleep to the news. I thought I heard something about another Ebola outbreak in Africa as I drifted off.

Screw Ebola. Who cared about panic-driven epidemic reports when you couldn't get it up?

# FOURTEEN

The first thing I did the next morning was destroy my cell phone. I snuck out of bed, Candy snoring lightly, and padded down to the garage. I wrapped a thick cloth around the phone and hammered away at it until I was pretty sure it was toast.

"Fuck you, AO," I seethed.

I went back inside and found the family iPad, breaking it in half over my knee. A part of me cringed, thinking of the money wasted. That shit wasn't cheap.

But I was done with AO, whoever it was. Sure, for some reason, AO had some scary yet bizarre ability to control me and force me to do things I didn't want to do. But that was only once I'd answered AO's call or text. If I could destroy AO's means of communication, I would stop being sucked into the murderous sickness.

Damn, it had felt good, taking down that fucking would-be school shooter, his white trash mother, and that dickweed road hog. I couldn't deny the intense feeling of elation that trilled through me when I snuffed them out. It felt...righteous.

All the more reason to put a stop to this—now!

I was going to avoid all electronics today. Even the radio and TV were off limits. I'd tell Candy and Katie that I wanted a special day to spend with them, with no distractions. We would go for a walk, play in the yard, break out the board games under Katie's bed. Time to get back to the *Little House on the Prairie* days. Charles Ingalls would never have been possessed by AO. No, sir. And not me anymore.

I was just hiding the TV remotes on the top bookshelf in the living room when Katie waltzed down the stairs rubbing her eyes.

"Hi, Daddy," she said. "Do I have to go to school today?"

"No, honey, not today," I replied, picking her up. "We're going to have a lot of fun. You want to help me make blueberry pancakes?" Maine was filthy with blueberries. Everywhere we looked, someone was selling blueberries out of their front yard. Thankfully, my daughter couldn't get enough of them.

Her face lit up, casting aside the drowsiness of sleep. "Yes! Can I do all the stirring?"

I walked her into the kitchen. "I'll even let you flip some."

She surprised me by kissing my stubbly cheek. "I like it when you don't work."

I kissed her back, smiling. "Me too. Now, you get the blueberries, and I'll get the pancake mix."

"Can we listen to Radio Disney?"

I paused. "Not today. Why don't you tell me a story while we cook?"

"What kind of story?" The pint of berries looked enormous in her tiny hands.

"Any kind. No, wait, make it a funny story."

"Like one about butts?" Katie giggled. She had recently discovered the word *butt* and there was no end to the fascination it held for her.

"Sure, a butt story will be perfect."

We cooked and talked about an angry butt that coughed farts. It was sick and so smelly, no one wanted to take it to the doctor. As I genuinely laughed at her potty humor tale, I couldn't stop wondering what she would think if she knew the very bad things her father had done. Would she be afraid of me? Would she run to her mother, pleading with her to send the bad man away?

Or would she still love me, not caring a whit about my recent bout with insanity?

Above all, that thought disturbed me the most. I'd become a monster, whether I liked it or not. I didn't want to know my child could love a monster.

The sweet aroma of pancakes brought Candy down from her slumber and I proposed my day of being unplugged. She nearly choked me out when she hugged her arms around my neck.

It was a good day, despite the strange silence of the neighborhood when we took our walk. The only vehicle that passed by what was usually a relatively busy Route 302 was a lumber truck, rattling past well over the speed limit, the stack of logs on the flatbed threatening to topple off. We had the park to ourselves, then went home and played Frisbee in the backyard.

Later that night, Candy and I again tried to make love, but it just wasn't happening. She said all the right things while I brooded in our darkened bedroom.

I fell asleep feeling like a hollow man. It wasn't just

the fact that I couldn't get it up that had scooped out some vital part of my being. That strange, telltale heat reddened my palms and legs as I tried to force sleep to come. I'd just had a near perfect day. After being a desk jockey for years, the amount of physical exercise I'd engaged in should have wiped me out.

Something had been missing.

My stomach lurched when I peeked into the black corners of my mind. I knew exactly why I was feeling unfulfilled.

I hadn't killed a single person.

And it was eating me alive.

# FIFTEEN

I took a trip the next afternoon to the library to do some job hunting after lying to Candy that I couldn't find the iPad. She packed a legal pad, two pens, highlighter, and a bag lunch. "Good luck, honey," she said, the look in her eyes filled with hope that my finding a job would ease my issues...down there.

Like the streets and shops, the library was empty save a young librarian with hair dyed pink at the tips. There was a growing tension not just in Bridgton, but it seemed everywhere. When you're a fledgling killer with impotency issues, you tend not to pay attention to very much outside your crumbling self, but it was getting impossible to avoid.

"Do I need to reserve time on the computer?" I asked.

The librarian looked around the room with an arched eyebrow. "It's all yours. You're the first person that's come in here all week. I don't even know why *I'm* here. Things are getting kinda scary, you know? I just keep telling myself that nothing bad ever happens in a library."

I wondered if she'd ever read Stephen King's *It*. Of course, that was fiction.

I snagged copies of *The Bridgton News*, the town's weekly, and *The Portland Press Herald* before settling behind the library's computer. The monitor was big and boxy and out of date by about a century. While I waited for the desktop to boot up, I scanned *The Bridgton News*.

The normally idyllic town had become a nest of crime. Between the main articles and the police blotter, I counted four homicides, three suicides, and seventeen assaults. This from a place where the biggest crime was usually people speeding off from the gas station without paying. The paper said the State Police were going to assign several cops to the town to assist the locals.

The *Herald* was much the same thing, though it encompassed a wider swath of towns.

"Jesus H. Christ," I muttered, fumbling through the pages.

There, on page three, was my handiwork.

MANHUNT STILL ON FOR ACCOMPLICE IN POTENTIAL SCHOOL SHOOTING

It appeared that the Saco police had come to the conclusion that the crazy ass kid I'd killed must have had a partner in crime. Said partner either had second thoughts about laying waste to the school or wanted all the glory for himself. Police were busy interrogating every student in the high school, which was leading to some serious unrest with the kids and their parents. Who the hell were the cops to come barging in, assuming their kids were stone-cold killers?

To my utter shock and surprise, I felt a world-class hard-on tenting my jeans. My groin area was stoked so hot, I could have fried an egg on the tip of my dick.

What the hell was wrong with me?

In fact, the more stories of murder and mayhem I read—and they were everywhere—the hotter and harder I got. Mixed in with police reports were more stories about a potential Ebola outbreak in Nebraska. Also, some kind of flu epidemic was sweeping through San Francisco at a time when no one should have the flu. I plopped my briefcase over my lap just in case the cute librarian walked by. The last thing I needed her to see was my erection while I was surrounded by open pages filled with nightmares.

The fever heat worked its way outward until I thought I was going to spontaneously combust. Oddly enough, I wasn't sweating. I kept wiping my forehead, expecting my hand to come away dripping.

Setting the newspapers aside, I opened up my Facebook account without thinking why I'd check something so nonsensical when all of this insane shit was going down.

The little Facebook message box that blinked on the bottom right of the screen gave me my answer.

Even though I had no friends with the initials AO, there was his message, waiting. I enlarged the message box. The text bubble sprouted from AO's image, which was a picture of a roaring flame.

**AO: I see you're starting to come around.**

*I typed:* **What the hell are you?**

I pushed my chair back from the computer. My

briefcase slipped off my lap. The sound was like a thunderclap in the silent library.

I had asked AO *what* it was instead of *who*. Why had I done that? Did a part of me know better? A *what* could be a tumor, the perfect alibi. A *who*, now that would be trouble. The tried and true mother's lament, *would you jump off a bridge if Jimmy told you to?*, could not excuse me from what I'd done.

**AO: Do you want to tamp out the fire?**

*I typed:* **You know I do, so why ask?**

It felt as if my flesh was going to melt from my bones. In another minute, I'd start stripping and the cops would be called to haul me away. Not that they had time to waste with a nude man in a library. What other horrors were being committed behind closed doors right now?

What horror could *I* be doing, right now? Just thinking about it dialed up the heat. I thought I smelled roasting pork and wondered if it was me.

**AO: This is bigger than the others. You have to want it.**

*I typed:* **Just tell me what it is. I'll do it.**

**AO: There's no return from this point on.**

*I typed:* **How the hell can I go back from what I've already done?**

There was a long, uncomfortable pause. I wiped some saliva from my mouth with the back of my hand. It stung like acid.

**AO: The Mustang is parked behind the library. There are two cases in the back seat. You need to use what's inside each case.**

I read on as AO dictated my marching orders.

It was awful. Unthinkable. For a moment, I thought I was going to pass out.

As the sun peeked through the windows behind me, I caught my reflection in the monitor's glare.

Despite everything I was feeling, I was smiling.

Smiling like the devil on a feast day.

I didn't go back home to Candy or try to call her at the town's last remaining pay phone. The Mustang ate the road like a man whose hunger strike had just ended. My hands should have been shaking, but they were steady on the wheel.

I had two destinations today. The first was in Portland. The second would be in New Hampshire. I figured the round trip would take me four to five hours. I could be home just in time for dinner.

If I had an appetite.

The agonizing heat had subsided the moment I sat in the car, but it was still there, a humming undercurrent like the thrum of a nuclear reactor.

At a light in Raymond, I leaned back and opened the two cases. The first one had my trusty scimitar. It should have been stained with crusty blood, but the blade shone like it was newly minted.

The other case contained an Uzi along with a half dozen magazines.

If I were a real man, I would take that Uzi, press it to the side of my head, and pull the trigger.

*If I were a real man.* I wasn't even sure what I was anymore. After this day, I wouldn't qualify as the worst speck of humanity's garbage.

So why was I so willing to go ahead with it?

It had to be more than just a Pavlovian aversion to the pain AO could inflict on me, right?

I made it to Portland, lost in my thoughts. I drove down narrow side streets that were totally unfamiliar to me. I kept expecting AO to speak to me through the car's speakers again.

Maybe even AO wanted to distance himself, or itself, from me on this one. Generals rarely rode into battle side by side with their troops.

I stopped outside the parking lot of a blue-domed building. Just like Bridgton, the state's largest city was a ghost town. A few people walked the streets but with wary faces.

The sun was unencumbered by clouds and the caw of seagulls echoed down tight alleys.

Staring at the building through the windshield, I thought it was probably empty, just like everyplace else. If it was, I was going to turn around and head home. Screw New Hampshire. The silence of this place would be a sign. A sign to stop this madness. Maybe I would introduce my head to the Uzi.

There was a smattering of cars in the lot and I saw a light in one of the windows of the mosque.

I took a deep breath, removing the scimitar and Uzi from their cases.

Practically running to the front door, I offered a silent prayer for my soul, expecting zero mercy.

# UNTHINKABLE

# SIXTEEN

There were only a dozen or so people in the mosque. All were men who appeared to be middle-aged and older. I shot nine with the Uzi, beheaded two with the scimitar, and let one run from the building, shrieking as if his mind had come unhinged.

My nerves were steady during the slaughter, which only added to my disgust. But the part of me screaming to stop was tamped deeper and deeper into the bowels of my soul. It was as if I were working on some kind of sadistic autopilot, only I knew exactly who the pilot was in this case.

AO.

When I was done, I casually walked back to the car, packed my weapons in their cases, and drove for New Hampshire, obeying the speed limit, in no particular rush. I didn't need the navigation system or AO instructing me where to go now. I was operating on pure instinct.

What I had done was unconscionable. Murdering people while they worshipped in what was supposed to be the sanctity of their faith. I had easily slipped past being a monster. I was a demon. I was the goddamn devil!

Driving down I-95, I saw tiny tendrils of smoke rising from the steering wheel. My first thought was to pull over and find out what was wrong with the car.

It wasn't the car.

The heat emanating from my palms was burning so hot, they were melting the wheel.

I cast a glance in the rearview mirror. The whites of my eyes had been replaced by black-veined rubies.

"What the fuck is happening to me?"

I also realized I was harder than a fire hydrant. It felt as if I were becoming something else, transforming into the unearthly creature I had doomed myself to become by my actions.

The moment I thought of taking an exit and turning back, my brain mushroomed. The Mustang swerved back onto the road. My head keranged off the side window.

I couldn't go home. First, because there was more to be done. Second, I couldn't let Candy and Katie see me like this. I wasn't their husband and father anymore. How could I be? My cock pulsated when I thought about mowing down innocent people in prayer. My hands could melt glass.

All I wanted to do was cry, but the tears wouldn't come—couldn't come.

The radio clicked on by itself. A newsman reported on the multiple quarantines being enforced in major cities around the country. What they thought was Ebola was actually some new virus that mimicked the disease but in turn was twice as deadly. It was spreading at an alarming rate. Worse still, it was now confirmed to be an airborne disease. The mortality rate was just under ninety percent. The CDC's resources were stretched thinner than the finest thread.

At the current rate of infection, it would jump from metropolitan centers to outlying areas in days, if not hours.

Was I driving into an infected zone?

That wouldn't have been a bad thing. Fate would have to be the one to stop me in my tracks, sending a microscopic bug into my system, killing me quickly, painfully. I was the dreaded martians in *The War of the Worlds*, weaving a path of destruction, a Goliath waltzing right into the tiniest David.

Another story caught my distracted attention just as I was crossing the border into New Hampshire. A freak storm had hammered the Midwest overnight, demolishing countless vital crops. Hurricanes had also popped up in Florida, wiping out orange groves as easily as a kid holding a magnifying glass over an ant farm.

Everything was coming unglued.

The car stopped of its own accord in Portsmouth.

"No," I said, staring at the high-spired church. "Not again. Please, not again."

AO's voice blared from the speakers, rattling my ribs, threatening to shred my eardrums.

"YES, AGAIN. WITHOUT IT, ALL WAS FOR NOTII-ING. DO IT NOW!"

My head ached; my flesh sizzled. And no matter how much I didn't want to do it, I found myself exiting the car, weapons in hand.

*Please, someone see the madman with the gun and*

*Arabic sword and call the police! Make sure you get a cop with an anxious trigger finger. Shoot me! Kill me now before I ruin the lives of everyone in the church!*

The big double doors squealed on hinges in desperate need of oil. An organ played, singing to the heavens with massive pipes bursting with fervent air. Walking down the aisle, I looked up to see the adult choir practicing. Men and women holding songbooks before them sang their hearts out.

*"Be not afraid, I go before you always..."*

I used to sing that very same song when I was a kid in the choir, two years before I was eligible to be an altar boy. When I was a kid, I loved just being in a church. It was so peaceful, so comforting. In church, I felt safe, cared for.

Now I was here to desecrate it.

I smelled something sharp and metallic.

My hand was cooking the handle of the Uzi!

The choir didn't even know I was in the church. How could they? The organ was playing loud enough to be heard in space.

Turning the gun on myself proved impossible. Not only wouldn't my hand cooperate, but my spirit, if I even had one anymore, was anxious to make the singing stop—forever.

I stepped farther down the center aisle to better see everyone in the choir. A man saw me, looked right at me as if to say *just one more chorus and I'll be right with you.*

The first barrage of bullets wiped the flesh from his face, spraying fragments of bone into the stained-glass window behind him. My arm swept from left to right, sparing no one. The organist slammed into the keys, bouncing off the organ and flipping over the rail. He landed at my feet, badly wounded, but alive.

"Allahu Akbar," I said, knowing I had a shit-eating grin on my face.

I pulled away from the church just as I heard the first sirens wailing.

One more stop.

There was a synagogue a few miles down the road. I'd never been to Portsmouth, but somehow I knew damn well about the synagogue. I just needed to spread my charm there and I could punch out for the day.

My clothes smoldered. Even my hair smelled the way it did when it got caught in a blow dryer.

Some people burned in hell for their sins.

It looked like I was getting an early start.

# SEVENTEEN

I drove back to Bridgton with Armageddon on my heels.

Surprisingly, I hadn't gotten a drop of blood on me, even though I'd just murdered several dozen people, setting off what was sure to be a New England holy war. It was almost as if someone were looking out for me. Yeah, right. The Uzi had jammed in the synagogue, so I'd had to finish the rest with the scimitar, leaving a lone survivor to spread the word.

Spread the word?

I didn't even know what the hell *the word* was supposed to be: that a maniac had come to town and decided to make it his own killing field?

According to the radio, I wasn't the only problem facing the country at the moment. What I'd done wasn't small potatoes, but it was still pretty substantial.

"Not even an attaboy from you, AO?" I shouted in the car. I felt like I could shoot flames from my eyes and fingertips, like something out of an Iron-Maiden-fueled fantasy. I'd done everything AO had ordered me to do—most of it with a sick glee that made me want to run from myself.

And now I was going home to my family. A demon on fire, looking to spend some quality time with my daughter and a nice, hot dinner. Oh yeah, the hotter the better.

*"They were all hypocrites."*

The voice carried over the radio, the DJ talking about a mass murder at a Portland mosque. Muslims as far away as the Middle East were already promising vengeance. The bodies were still warm and sabers were rattling.

I realized that AO's voice wasn't coming through the car's speakers. I turned the radio off.

"What did you say?"

*"Hypocrites. All of them. Poseurs of the worst kind. They were all representative of the cancer that has festered within their faiths for far too long. You have nothing to feel sorry about."*

AO was in my head now. Odds are, he always had been.

I looked down at my lap. Obviously my cock wasn't feeling the slightest twinge of regret. It could have doubled as a maypole. I was pretty sure that if I undid my jeans, I would see an appendage far bigger than the one I'd been working with all my life. Blood ran through my groin like magma.

"Those were innocent people," I said, swerving around a truck to get into the left lane. A black pillar of smoke billowed out from the tops of the trees to my left. The steady bleat of sirens charged the late afternoon air.

*"No, not a one."*

"That's easy for you to say. You're not the one doing the killing. What I did isn't going to stop there. It's going to ignite a damned holy war! And I left witnesses! My face is going to be on every news channel. You had me kill a school shooter and avoid a catastrophe, only to make me the worst kind of mass murderer. What I did isn't going to stop there. Just like in Bridgton, it only spurs people to do bad shit!"

The wheel turned of its own accord, breaking my hot grip. The Mustang cut across three lanes of traffic, settling onto the shoulder of the highway.

*"You don't tell me what is and what isn't easy! You have no concept of the amount of pain and loss I feel! I suffer not just the now, but what has gone before and what is to come."*

"Cry me a river. You're just a voice in my head. When I get electrocuted for this, you won't even feel a spark." I was breathing awfully heavy. My emotions were riding a high wire. I was seething with anger at the same time I was disgusted, terrified as well as reveling in the power a voice, car, and two weapons had given me.

"Just let me get back on the road so I can see my wife and child for the last time."

I tried to turn the wheel, but it didn't budge.

"Come on, AO old buddy, I'm not kidding around! I don't think I have much time left outside a prison cell. For all I know, a squadron of cops is waiting for me to get home. They'll probably shoot me on sight. All I ask is that I get to see Candy and Katie one more time, even if it's from a distance."

The wheel suddenly stopped fighting me.

Wow, for once AO had done something I'd told him to do instead of the other way around. Maybe I was finally gaining control of myself.

A day late and a dollar short.

If my sanity was returning, it was just in time to watch my life spin down the toilet.

I thought of several excuses I could give Candy for being out all day. I'd decide which one to use when I saw her, feeling her out. If I wasn't going to be gunned down on my front lawn, I just wanted to hold her and Katie. That is, if I could get my core body temperature down. If they were with me now, I'd give them third-degree burns.

The redness was leaching from my eyes. It seemed the closer I got to Bridgton, the more my humanity returned. I kept the radio off. I'd heard and seen enough today. Talk about killer diseases couldn't penetrate the scenes in my head—bullets tearing through people, the explosions of tattered flesh, muscle, and blood, limbs twitching on the floor after I'd carved them with the scimitar. Heads bouncing like stinky pinky balls.

And the cries, the pleading, the wails of agony moments before I ended their misery. Christ. They would plague me the rest of my days, which was all the more reason to hope there weren't many left in the life bank.

Turning onto my block, disappointment and elation at not seeing a sign of any police played tug of war. I pulled the Mustang into my driveway. There was no sense hiding it at this point.

My forehead smashed into the front door when I

turned the knob in full stride. It was locked. Candy never locked the door during the day. It was part of the appeal of moving up to Maine.

I checked my pockets for my keys, relieved that my body had cooled considerably. The door whooshed open. Candy looked at me and broke down crying. She tugged me into the house by my shirt collar, closing the door behind me.

"Thank God you're home," she said, sobbing into my chest.

Confused, I put my arms around her.

"What happened? Is Katie all right?" I said.

"Haven't you seen the news?" Her eyes were bloodshot and puffy. "That virus, or whatever it is, is spreading like wildfire. Peter, my mother called two hours ago. She and Dad were going to the hospital because they think they have it. They've been running high fevers and vomiting nonstop since last night. She said she'd call me right back and I haven't heard from her. Every time I call, I get a message that all the circuits are busy. I...I'm going crazy not knowing where they are or what's wrong with them."

Candy's parents lived all the way in Arizona. It wasn't as if we could just hop in the car to check on them.

"I'll go look at flights," I said.

She held me so hard I couldn't take a step. "You can't. The FAA grounded all flights an hour ago."

"Are you kidding me? What are we, at war?"

This was bad. Real bad. Maybe so bad that I would get away with all of my crimes. When things were so screwed that travel was suspended and martial law enacted, a few shootings could easily slip into the cold case files quickly.

But people had seen me. I hadn't even had the sense to wear a ski mask.

Candy sniffled. "The government wants to cease all travel to prevent this from becoming a pandemic. The only way we could get to my parents is by driving, and I'm pretty sure the highways are the next to be shut down."

I led her to the couch. "First, your parents are going to be all right. Remember when 9-11 happened? All of the phone lines were jammed. I couldn't get through to you all day. I guarantee your mother is trying to call right now but the circuits are busy."

That seemed to calm her a little, but she was still trembling with hysteria.

"If you want, I'll keep trying to call her every five minutes until I get through. Why don't you take a Xanax and settle down? When I do get through to your mother, it won't do her any good to hear her daughter freaking out."

Candy kissed my cheek, her tears falling onto my flesh.

"God, I love you," she whispered. "And you feel warm again. I hope you're not getting one of those fevers. I don't want to have to go to the emergency room. I bet it's filled with people who are either sick or think they are."

I cupped her face in my hands. "I'm fine. We're not going to the hospital. Where's Katie?"

"Upstairs playing."

"That's one good thing. I'll get the pill and some water."

Candy turned the TV on while I went to the medicine cabinet. I peeked in on Katie, who was putting on a cooking show with her little plastic kitchen set. Her audience was her stuffed animals, all lined up to watch her talk about how to make chocolate chip cookies. She didn't notice me.

As we sat on the couch flipping through all of the news channels, and every channel was now broadcasting live news feeds, I could see why Candy was a mess and so afraid for her parents.

It looked and sounded like the world was coming down around us—people getting sick in record numbers, looting, the military trying to get a lid on large cities, talk of food shortages, and strange weather patterns. And murders. Sweet Jesus, people were killing each other as if it were a video game and a billion dollars was the prize.

Who was I to be shocked by that? On one local channel, they briefly mentioned the shooting at the mosque. I guess the other two holy institutions didn't rate. My stomach clenched when the talking head said the police had a sketch of the shooter. I tried to grab the remote from Candy's hands to change the channel. I noticed, too late, that it had slipped between the cushion and the couch.

A black-and-white drawing of what looked like a middle-aged rabbi flashed on the screen.

*"If you recognize the man in this photo, the police are urging that you call their tip line at..."*

What the hell?

The poor schmuck in the sketch didn't look a thing like me. How could the guy I'd let live come up with that?

Candy stared at the TV, numb now, thanks to both the information overload and tranquilizer.

Then it hit me.

Someone *was* looking out for me.

AO.

Which meant, he wasn't in my head at all.

# EIGHTEEN

I hadn't been able to sleep at all. Katie came, sleepy-eyed, into our bedroom around two, settling between us. She'd had a nightmare and fell asleep before she could tell me what it was about.

My mind was a whirling dervish.

AO was real. He had to be. And he had complete and total control over me. I mean, I should have been snatched by the police by now. Not once did I ever try to hide my face or actions. I just jumped in the most conspicuous car in the state and mowed people down with a semi-automatic and a damn scimitar. When people saw me, and there had to be more witnesses than I even knew about, what did they see? Did they all see a meek rabbi? Or did some see a Hispanic man with a scar atop one eye or a plump Chinese guy with long hair and horn-rimmed glasses? It sounded ridiculous, but I was beginning to think that when it came to AO, anything was possible.

AO had gotten me to kill, forcing pain on me until I did his bidding. And somehow, in the process of becoming a mass murderer, I was morphing into something else, something that was not me at all.

And now AO could talk to me anywhere and any time he wanted. I stiffened at the thought of him speaking as my family slept beside me. Would they be able to hear him now, too? Did he gain strength as the world weakened?

For the first time since I was a kid, I prayed. When I said every prayer I could remember, skipping some lines, messing up others, I said them again, tears silently leaking from my eyes. I prayed until the sun came up, knowing it would never be enough.

"We need milk and bread and some other things, but I'm afraid to leave the house," Candy said. Katie sat on my lap, trying to get me to be silly with her. I was a zombie. I could barely comprehend what she was saying.

"Wh-what?" I asked, running Katie's hair through my fingers.

Candy had her phone in her hand, hitting the speed dial for her mother. Since yesterday the "all circuits are busy, please hang up and call again" message had played in a maddening loop. "I said we're running out of the food basics. But I don't think it's safe for any of us to leave the house."

While we slept, the last vestiges of normalcy had simply slipped away. Over the course of nine hours, chaos had been given an inch and taken a yard. People were urged, no, ordered, to stay in their homes. The National Guard had been called to so many places, there was no way they could be everywhere they were needed. Cities were burning from looters. First responders were lying in overcrowded hospitals, felled by a contagion that had yet to be named, but had done more damage in less time than the great influenza epidemic of 1918. Hurricanes battered the southern coasts on both sides and tornadoes popped up in places that had never seen a twister.

"I'll go," I said.

"No, Daddy, stay here and play with me. Can you get Elefun from my closet?"

"I will when I get back, sweetie," I said, transferring her to a chair.

The phone beeped as Candy hung up. She'd slept like a log, but there were dark circles under her eyes. "She's right, Peter. Stay here. We can make do. You shouldn't go outside anyway. It's not safe."

I looked out the window. I didn't even see our morning squirrels tightrope walking on the phone lines.

"Do we have milk and chocolate powder?" I asked.

"No but—"

"Katie needs her chocolate milk, don't you?"

Katie considered it for a moment, then nodded. Chocolate milk was a life necessity in her eyes. And she wasn't aware of what was really going on outside. But she was smart enough to read our vibes, and they weren't good.

"See," I said. "There's no choice. Make a list and I'll make a run to Hannaford's."

Sighing, Candy said, "I don't like this at all." Whispering, she added, "I'm scared, Peter. I thought I heard someone screaming before. What's happening?"

I bent close to her face so our noses were touching. "I don't know, honey. But this may be our last chance to get the stuff we need for a while. We may need to hole up in the basement when I get back, ride things out until help comes. Bring whatever you can downstairs, including extra batteries and the radio."

We flinched when we heard the crunch of metal echoing outside. I looked but couldn't see the crash. Candy grabbed my hand, her own trembling.

"Please, stay. What if there are people in the super-market that are sick?"

"I'll keep to myself. Go on, make that list. I gotta get changed. After this, we circle the wagons, okay?"

She reluctantly went back to the kitchen, grabbing the magnetic pad off the fridge and a pen. I went upstairs and slipped on a new pair of jeans, black T-shirt, and baseball cap.

I had to get out of the house. Somehow, despite the growing madness, I knew no harm would come to me.

There was one stop I absolutely needed to make.

# TRUTH

# NINETEEN

The first thing I noticed was that the Mustang was gone. I assumed it had slunk off on its own, lying in wait like a lion until it was needed again.

I made a quick stop before the supermarket, saw the oak doors were locked and read the plaque installed in the masonry. With any luck, it would be open when I was done with the shopping.

Shopping. It seemed impossible to be doing something so mundane when I had so much blood on my hands. Mass murderers aren't supposed to casually head to the store for milk and Cheerios.

The Hannaford parking lot was almost empty. This time of day, it should have been at least half full. This was when the retirees came out to shop, and there were plenty of them in town to fill the aisles. I used to tell Candy shopping on a weekday morning was like being cast as an extra in *The Walking Dead*. Except the zombies in the show moved faster.

But this was no ordinary day. I'd passed several car accidents on my way to the store, no signs of drivers anywhere. Someone had driven a truck into the little gazebo ice cream stand. The flavor of the day was dripping oil and radiator fluid.

I was punched in the nose by the stench of rotting fruit and vegetables the moment I stepped into the store. The produce section was right inside the front sliding doors. What little food was left on the shelves had gone to seed. Overturned boxes labeled for bananas and lettuce littered the floor. It was safe to assume they weren't getting any new shipments and the produce manager had called it quits.

Turning to my left, I saw there was one person working the registers, an older woman with dyed red hair. A lit cigarette dangled from her mouth as she scanned the groceries for a nervous-looking couple. I heard her say, "I don't even know why I'm doing this. It's not like I'm going to charge you."

The man replied, "Please, I want to pay for it."

"Why bother? The charge machine has been down for days and my till has no change. People have just been taking what they want and running for days. I'm just here because it beats staying at home and watching the news."

Pushing my cart past the empty boxes, I stepped in a black, mushy banana and almost took a header. How vaudevillian that would have been. I wasn't amused.

The rest of the store was a mess. The shelves were pretty damn bare. All of the medicine and first-aid supplies were gone. I wasn't shocked to see the wine and alcohol aisle had been completely wiped out. There wouldn't be milk or any fresh dairy today. I grabbed whatever random cans and boxes of food I could find. A scattering of people did the same, leaning on their carts, shuffling as if in a dream.

I thought, this is what a market must look like the day after a bombing. Opportunists had stripped the place bare, and those late birds were left to wander around, too shocked to care that the only thing they'd bring home were canned beets and a jar of jellied gefilte fish.

As far as I could tell, the old redhead was the only one working in the entire store.

Coming to the small section dedicated to books and magazines, I had to stifle a laugh. Those shelves looked as if they'd been recently stocked. I shouldn't have been surprised. People barely read anymore when times were good. Why escape with a book when you could be glued to the catastrophe on television?

I grabbed a copy of *Highlights* for Katie, along with a coloring book and a sticker book. My legs locked when I heard an ungodly scream from the next aisle over. A woman scooted past me, anxious to get away from the screamer. Maybe I should have followed suit, but I had to see what was going on.

A man lay on the floor, his body convulsing. Blood seeped from his eyes while white foam bubbled from his mouth.

"Aaaiiiiieeee, I'm burning! Somebody help me!"

Sweet Jesus, was this what the infection was like that was ravaging the country? I thought of my own condition, feeling as if I were on fire, passing out and convulsing that night in front of Candy. Was I a carrier? Or were my symptoms really the result of AO trying to keep me in line?

Either way, I couldn't help him. Not if it meant

bringing what he had back to Candy and Katie. I started to steer away from him as his back arched, hands thrown out at his sides. One of them flicked the bottom shelf, causing the lone bottle of ketchup to fall and shatter. The back of his hand impaled on the broken glass. I couldn't tell where his blood began and the ketchup ended.

"I'm...I'm sorry," I whispered, heading for the register.

I pulled up to the redhead. She eyed the meager contents of my cart.

"No sense taking them out, hon," she said.

"There's a man over there. I think he's dying."

She shrugged. "He's not the first. Except I don't have anyone around to clean up today. I guess there are worse places to go."

Her cavalier attitude both rocked me and settled my frayed nerves.

"Should you call an ambulance?" I asked.

"No one's going to come," she replied, lighting another cigarette with the glowing end of her current smoke. "Or haven't you seen the news?"

She handed me some reusable shopping bags. "Here, you can use these. I'm closing up here soon. I don't think I'll be coming back. My sister is in a nursing home over in Naples. I think I'll go stay with her, if they'll let me. You have family here?"

I slowly nodded. She saw the children's magazine atop my tiny haul.

"You go home to your kid. There's no sense coming out anymore. At least not until things settle down or the military comes in and gets things straight again."

I gripped the cart's handle until my knuckles

whitened. "I will. And...good luck getting to your sister. I'm sure she'll appreciate it very much."

The woman took a quick drag. "She hasn't known who I am for two years now. But I know my Linda." Her gaze drifted off, staring out the front windows to someplace I'd never be able to see. "I know my Linda."

I got to my car just as a black rain cloud slipped over the parking lot. The ugly, pregnant cloud looked so out of place in the blue sky. There wasn't another like it in any direction.

Balls of hail smacked the car as I pulled out of the driveway. The storm followed me all the way back to my next stop.

# TWENTY

It had been a long time since I had been in a church. Well, at least a church I wasn't shooting up.

I was a little surprised to find the door unlocked. The whole country had gone to shit and flown the coop, literally or figuratively. Priests were only human, flesh and blood with all the same flaws as everyone else. I figured any priest with half a brain would either hunker down in the parish house and pray for it all to end or hit the road in search of all the forbidden fruit he could find.

St. Mark's Church smelled like candle wax and wood polish, scents I always associated with well-being and peace. The silence in the small church was as calming as it was unnerving. A little sign in the narthex listed the daily mass schedule. There should have been a mass going on right now. If my altar boy memories were correct, the priest would be on to the gospel reading, if there were anyone to read to.

"Hello," I called out.

A crucified Jesus, hung behind the altar, stared back

at me. As a kid, I used to feel such sorrow, such intense awe when I looked at the face of Jesus on the cross. Now I felt like the accused. Did his eyes narrow, just a bit?

I sat in the last pew, avoiding Jesus's gaze. I contemplated kneeling, maybe saying some prayers, but that wasn't why I had come here.

The wood cracked as I got up. I walked down the red runner in the center aisle. A little table had been set up for the holy gifts, the wine and the unconsecrated Eucharist. I brushed a layer of dust off the empty tabletop as I passed. I started to make the sign of the cross when I got to the altar, stopping midway. Who was I to bless myself? I didn't deserve it.

"Is anyone here?"

There was a half-empty glass of water on the pulpit. There wouldn't be readings here any time soon, if ever.

The sound of a door opening made me jump. A bald, portly man wearing a black shirt and wrinkled slacks came in through the door to my left. He peeked out from beside a statue of Mary standing on a pedestal.

"Can I help you?" he said. He looked nervous as if my presence could only be a bad omen. If only he knew who had come to visit.

"Are you a priest?" I asked.

He nodded. "I'm Father Brendan. If you've come for mass, I wasn't planning on it today. Perhaps Sunday, if..."

His voice and gaze trailed off to a place of wishful thinking.

"I'm not here for mass."

"Oh."

I stayed perfectly still, letting him see my hands were empty. I was sure the news of the church massacre weighed heavily on him. I was a stranger in a strange time. He had every right to be wary.

"Father, would you be able to hear my confession?"

His shoulders sagged with relief.

"Yes, of course I would. You're the first person to come to me and ask. I prefer to think that my congregation is too afraid to leave their homes. Strange to be consoled thinking that the people I hold dear are paralyzed in fear. It's too disheartening to think they've all lost their faith when they need it most."

I nodded. "I'm sure they're hunkered down. Things aren't good out there."

Father Brendan motioned toward a pew. "Please, have a seat. I can hear your confession here."

I couldn't imagine facing the man, telling him what I'd done. It was going to be hard enough just to say the words.

"I'd prefer the confessional, if that's okay with you," I said. A lone confessional was tucked away in the back corner of the church. Both doors were open.

"I understand."

"It's just that it's been a long time, and that's the way I grew up doing it," I explained, but I could see in his eyes that there was no need.

"You take a seat. Let me get my clerical collar so we do this the right way. It's not as if I have anything else pressing to do for the rest of the day."

He left the church in a hurry, his legs carrying his round body faster and more surefooted than I would have expected. I took a deep breath and walked to the confessional, closing the door behind me. Inside was dark and silent, like being in the womb of the church itself.

Alone with my thoughts, I almost bolted. What the hell was I thinking? Father Brendan seemed like a nice enough guy. Why burden him with my guilt? Just so I could feel better about myself? Was absolution so important that I had to destroy another man in the process? There was no way he could hear my confession and not come out a changed man. Would it destroy him, knowing who the monster of Maine was and not be able to tell another soul?

I was about to get out, run from the church, when I heard the door on the other side of the confessional close. Neither of us spoke. I had forgotten what I was supposed to say. Father slid the tiny door open in the window separating us. The window was screened with black lattice so I couldn't see him. He was just a vague, dark shape.

Meager light from his side bled through the partition. I looked down, seeing a laminated card taped to a narrow shelf. It had the words and order of confession. It was hard to see, but I read them as best I could.

"Bless me, Father, for I have sinned. It's been...I don't know, fifteen years since my last confession."

Father Brendan replied, "In the name of the Father, the Son, and the Holy Spirit."

I mumbled the same, waiting for him to give me some kind of cue. There was so much I needed to say, so much I hated myself for, I didn't know where to start.

*Father Brendan, I'm the guy who murdered over fifty people over the past week. How many Hail Marys is that gonna cost?*

I thought, maybe he's having second thoughts about this. Maybe he's lost the faith, just like the members of his church.

Fuck it.

"Father, I've committed some very serious sins."

My hands clasped together and I kneeled. A tremor ran through my body.

"Go on," he urged, his voice low and gravelly.

"I...I've killed."

There was no inward hiss of shock on the other side of the partition. He didn't shout at me, threatening to call the cops. No, he stayed perfectly quiet.

"It all started when I was let go from my job. Something came over me, and I killed my boss right outside his house. And...and when I was done, I went home to my family and acted as if nothing had happened."

"Did you tell anyone what you had done?"

I choked back a sob. "No. But he wasn't the only one. Days later, I murdered a man who was molesting his son. The boy saw me do it, but I think it traumatized him so much, he wasn't able to properly describe me to the police. And it didn't stop there."

Telling him about the school shooter and his mom came out a little easier. Each confessed crime made me lighter. My breathing steadied. I had to pause before going into the church shootings, knowing this would really hit home with him. But I did it anyway, finishing with the massacre at the synagogue. When I was done, I was weak. My bones felt as if they'd morphed into overdone pasta. I leaned my head against the confessional wall. I'd never run a marathon, but I suspected this is what it felt like when you crossed the finish line.

Except there was no joy, no sense of accomplishment. I felt bare, exposed, sick with the anticipation of judgment.

Finally, Father Brendan said, "What drove you to commit these acts?"

I wanted to say "insanity!" That sounded better than telling him the texts on my computer and phone, the voice in the car and my head. But I had gone this far. There was no sense holding back now.

"I'm not sure," I said, wiping tears from my cheeks. "Someone or something that calls himself AO has been telling me what to do, providing the tools I need, punishing me when I disobey him. I don't know who he is or how he's found a way to control me, to torture me."

The seat creaked on the other side as if the priest were moving closer to the partition.

"I think you do know who this AO is," he said.

My head dropped down until my forehead touched my clasped hands.

"If he's real, how is he doing this to me? How can he get inside my head?"

"Because he is AO."

Something in Father Brendan's tone changed. My head jerked up.

"What does that mean?"

Father chuckled, chilling my blood. "It *has* been too long for you. All that religious education out the door traded for earthly desires and possessions." There was a long pause. All I could hear was my own labored breathing. "AO. He is the Alpha and the Omega, Peter."

How did he know my name? I was pretty sure I hadn't told him. I got up from my knees, sitting back on the padded chair.

"No," I croaked, feeling the confessional spin around me.

It wasn't possible.

*"You remember Revelation, don't you, Peter? 'When the lamb broke the second seal, I heard the second living creature saying, 'Come.' And another, a red horse, went out, a fiery red one. Its rider was given power to take peace from the earth, and that men would slay one another; and a great sword was given to him.'"*

Standing up, I fumbled for the knob. I had to get out.

"The red horseman is a harbinger of war and destruction. You've been chosen, Peter! Chosen to herald the end of corruption and the beginning of eternal peace! Listen to the Alpha and the Omega. Your soul rests in the bosom of the Lord God!"

"Noooo!"

I kicked the door open so hard it came off its hinges. My body ignited. It was as if I'd been doused in melted iron. Father Brendan continued spouting quotes from Revelation.

"God wouldn't do this to me!" I shouted back.

I was overcome by a desire to make the priest shut up in the most violent way possible. I found a heavy candle stand and grabbed it. I was going to put it in places that weren't meant to be explored.

Father Brendan, still inside the confessional, said, "Those worthy will drink from the water of life. Without you, Peter, they would not be able to testify, 'Yea, I am coming soon.'"

The air shook with the sound of a towering foghorn, an otherworldly rumble that came from the sky and buried itself into the earth. I stumbled back-ward, using the candle stand to keep from falling.

*What the hell was that?*

It should have terrified me, but my anger was far greater than my fear.

Grabbing the handle to the confessional, I yanked it open with a primal scream.

The candle stand dropped from my hand, clattering on the tiled floor.

It was empty.

How?

"Father Brendan?" I shouted.

He'd just been inside, screeching his insane holy words. I checked for any hidden ways out. My rage was so ebullient I tore the wooden confessional to pieces with my bare hands. Hunks of wood clattered every-where, smoking from where I'd touched them.

"Where are you, Father? I *am not* the red horseman! You hear me! I will not kill for God."

The words struck me, stopping me in my rage.

Wasn't I about to kill Father Brendan? In just a few days, killing had become easy, something I had yearned to do. I couldn't get it up for Candy, but given the chance to bury the scimitar in someone's flesh and I was in porn star territory. And now I was the human torch, tearing up a church, desperate to rip a priest to pieces just because I didn't like what he had to say.

My hands glowed red. My eyes burned, but I could see perfectly.

AO. The Alpha and the Omega. The Greek term for Christ, for God, the deliverer of the end times in the Book of Revelation.

I didn't want it to make sense.

I stormed down the main aisle, walking past the altar to the door where Father Brendan had come from earlier.

He was hanging by a white cassock in the sacristy. His swollen tongue filled his open mouth. The flesh of his face was blue, his eyeballs gray and bulging. His hanging wasn't fresh. Father Brendan had been dead for days. The stench of his fruiting body made me gag. I turned and ran.

The fresh air outside stung my burning body like nettles. I stopped on the top step.

Who had I been speaking to in the church if Father Brendan was dead?

AO.

The Alpha and the Omega. God.

What seemed impossible just minutes ago now felt all too real. I'd never been much for the Book of Revelation—that was a hyperbolic claptrap for half-mad Bible thumpers. I was a lapsed Catholic with a capital L. I was no horseman.

And yet, somehow, I was.

*Father Brendan's voice called out behind me. "How long, O Lord, must I call for your help, but you do not listen? Or cry out to you, 'Violence!', but you do not save?"*

I turned, but he was not there. He couldn't be. The man who had been Father Brendan was rotting at the end of a noose.

*"'Look at the nations and watch—and be utterly amazed. For I am going to do something in your day that you would not believe, even if you were told.'"*

The horn sounded again. The trees swayed from the soul-shaking bellow.

A strong wind battered the church, and within the wind, I heard the cries of men, women, and children.

My car was gone.

The red Mustang was in its place, the motor running, smoke belching from the tailpipe.

*Get in!*

It was the voice of AO. I clenched my fists.

"Just let me die!" I shouted.

*You know who I am. Do you trust in me?*

"Trust in you? How can I trust in a god who turns an innocent man into a killer? I'm not one of your horsemen. They come from heaven, or hell, I don't know! They don't come from here."

A part of me wanted to collapse and weep before the church, but a growing part wanted to obey AO, to let him take me wherever he desired.

Shots popped in the near distance. The smell of smoke drifted on the breeze.

*You have places far to go, with many days and nights without rest. Follow my words, and you will be saved.*

I couldn't reconcile the God I had prayed to as a child offering salvation for my soul through the act of murder. My legs walked to the car against my will. The concrete sizzled with each step.

Sitting in the car, I looked at myself in the rearview mirror.

My heart froze.

# TWENTY-ONE

I no longer looked human. My skin was as red as a ripe tomato. The whites of my eyes were crimson, the pupils a glowing gold. I watched in horror as the hair from my head burned off, black ash peppering my shoulders.

The scimitar was on the seat next to me, shining as if it had been recently polished. The back seat was crammed with cases and crates. All of them, I suspected, contained weapons, the tools to ignite mass murder.

Sitting in the Mustang, looking like the devil incarnate, I could no longer rationalize AO and what had been happening to me away. The less I struggled internally, the more the burning desire to carry out his word took control, easing my mind.

"I...I want to say goodbye to my family," I said, putting the car in drive.

*I am your family.*

"Candy and Katie are the family I made here, on Earth!" I shouted, pounding the wheel, feeling insane, raw power surge through me. If an army had been sent to stop me from going to my house, I was pretty sure I could lay waste to them, even without the scimitar. "You teach love. I love my wife and my child. It can't be wrong to love them so much that I want to see them one last time."

I pinned the accelerator. Route 302 was empty. It looked like there were several fires in the town. Smoke corkscrewed up from the tree line in every direction. There were no bleating fire engines rushing to the rescue.

The horns. They signaled the end. What little horror that had been held back must have exploded at the first blast. Everything had gone to total shit in an instant.

AO...no, God...didn't say another word as I sped to my house. When I pulled into the driveway, I saw my neighbor, Benny, lying dead on his front lawn. Blood pooled around his head. I didn't have time to find out what had happened to him.

Stepping out of the car, my point of view shifted. I was seeing the world from a different perspective. When I got to my front door, I realized I was taller than before. I would have to duck to get into the house. My frame nearly filled the doorway.

What was I doing? If Candy and Katie saw me like this, I might scare the life out of them.

Is this what God wanted, why he didn't stop me?

It was too late for second thoughts. The door swung open, the knob melting from my brief contact.

"Candy? Katie?"

Even my voice was deeper.

There was no answer. Had something happened? Had they run from the house? Maybe Benny had been trying to protect them from someone, or something. Or had they fled out the back door when they spotted me walking up the drive? I wouldn't blame them if they had.

Maybe it was for the best.

I turned for the front door, consigned to leaving my life and loves behind. Who was I to think I even deserved to see them again? Something wicked had to have lived in me all my life for God to choose me to be his messenger of war and hate. How could Candy have not seen it in me all these years?

The dying part of my soul wept.

My gaze caught something on the couch.

It was them. Both sound asleep in an unnatural slumber. They looked so peaceful, contented. I stood over them, Katie sleeping in the crook of Candy's arm. I exhaled with a big sigh when I saw their chests move. For a moment, I'd thought they were gone.

A heavy explosion rumbled through the house. Outside, a chorus of pained cries split the humid air.

Madness had taken complete control.

"Peter."

"Yes."

"You must leave them."

I reached out to touch them, saw the pulsating crimson in my hands, and pulled away.

"But first you must take their lives."

I recoiled, staggering away from the couch.

"You can't ask me to do that!"

Another blast made framed pictures fall from the walls. It felt as if something underground had erupted.

"If they live, they will suffer. The world will no longer be a place for them."

"Couldn't you just take them up? They're innocent. Please don't ask me to do this. I can't murder my wife and child."

*"You must trust in me."*

"Why would you make me do this? Haven't you done enough to torture me? I won't! Why me? Answer me that. Why me?"

To my surprise, I wasn't struck by pain, made to drop to my knees in agony until I acquiesced. Candy and Katie slept, oblivious to the chaos outside and the beast that was their protector inside.

*"They will feel nothing. Better that than the pain that is to come. Better from the hands of the one who loves them than a stranger."*

My tears hissed like droplets of water steaming on a hot plate.

*"This was always your burden to bear, Peter. I made you for this, an ordinary man in my image."*

My stomach lurched when I looked down and saw the scimitar in my right hand. I knew I had left it in the car.

"Please, spare them. Spare me. I'll do anything else you ask of me. Just don't ask me to do this."

Katie mumbled in her sleep, shifting so her face was nuzzled in Candy's breast. Candy pressed her cheek atop her head, a smile creeping onto her face.

*"You have much to do, but not until you place your absolute faith in me."*

"I do. I do have faith in you!"

*"Then believe in me when I say this has to be done."*

There were a series of gunshots just outside the house. A woman screamed and there were more shots. That could have been Candy. My chest ached.

If I left, whoever was out there could come into my home and do the same to my beautiful girls.

My beautiful, perfect girls.

"Please, forgive me," I said, sniffing back tears as I lifted the scimitar.

*"You need not ask me for forgiveness."*

"I'm not asking it of you!"

The scimitar sliced through the air as I screamed, a peal of lament that shattered windows, rending a path in the heavens for their souls to ascend.

# WORLD WITHOUT END

# TWENTY-TWO

The roads to D.C. were littered with smashed cars, people dead or dying of disease or wounds. The Mustang cleaved through them all as if they were nothing but phantoms.

I stopped at the gates to the White House. The black fence stood strong, its barrier secure as ever.

Three other Mustangs screeched to a halt beside me. One was black, the horseman known as famine. The scales of justice were emblazoned on its hood as if it had been detailed by one of those shops you saw on cable TV. Next to it was a white Mustang, the conquering horseman, the bringer of disease and pestilence. Even the windows were tinted white, a dense impenetrable fog. On the other side of my car was another Mustang, painted an unnatural pale that trailed a black, vaporous mist behind from its rumbling tailpipe. The pale horseman had frightened me as a child, because it was death, the most fearsome and final of us all. It scared me now, just idling beside it.

I couldn't see the drivers in any of the cars because

of the tinting, but I knew they were men, just like me. Had AO asked them to make the same final sacrifice?

It made me feel better to think he had. To know I wasn't alone in my sorrow, or my duty.

We had converged on this spot for just a moment, a respite from our work, a break from so much destruction. This would be our last stop here. I wasn't sure where we'd go next—Canada? Europe? The Middle East? Even great oceanic divides wouldn't stop us.

The white and black Mustangs peeled away, barreling in opposite directions, headed for their destinies.

I revved the engine, looking over at the pale Mustang. The black cloud undulated. If I stared hard, I could see inhuman shapes shifting within the venomous fog.

The pale horseman and I had work to do.

The sooner we got it done, the sooner I could once again be with my family. I screamed their names and revved the engine.

Together, the pale rider and I mowed the fence down, tearing up the Great Lawn for our meeting with the leader of the free, and damned, world.

# ACKNOWLEDGMENTS

Well, that was fun, wasn't it? Odd that this is the story that demanded to be written during the Christmas holiday.

There are so many people I'd like to thank not only for this book, but for everything I've been able to do, spinning yarns, for the past five years.

First, thank you to my first readers and editors—my sister, Carolyn Wolstencroft, who has been the eagle-eye first line editor for all my books; Jason Brant, a terrific writer, for giving me his thoughts and insight; and my wife, Amy, who never looks at me funny, no matter how demented the story.

Thank you to all the priests, nuns, and brothers who did their best to raise me right. You made writing stories like this one easy, because I don't need to spend weeks doing research. You taught me well and made sure everything stuck!

And to all of you who read this tale. Thank you for reading the voices in my head.

# A LOOK AT

## COMBUSTIBLE: A POST-APOCALYPTIC ROAD TRIP

**POST-APOCALYPTIC HORROR MEETS THRILLER IN A DYSTOPIAN NIGHTMARE OF FIRE AND ASH.**

The world didn't end with a bang or a whimper—it ended with people bursting into flames.

Across the globe, spontaneous human combustion (SHC) is turning ordinary citizens into living infernos. Governments collapse, cities fall silent, and the air itself tastes like ash. Society burns while the lucky few are left to wonder: When will it be me?

Sam and Aja were already falling apart before the fires came. Now, trapped in a crumbling apartment and suffocating under the weight of isolation, their love feels just as doomed as the rest of humanity. But when whispers spread of a small Canadian town called "Consumption", untouched by the inferno, hope flickers.

Stealing an RV and refusing to leave Aja behind, Sam sets out on a desperate, ash-streaked journey through a burned-out North America. With his best friend in tow and a growing crew of strange, unforgettable survivors, they chase rumors through a landscape warped by horror, madness, and the heat of human combustion.

*AVAILABLE NOW*

# ABOUT THE AUTHOR

Hunter Shea is a lifelong horror hound and writer of over thirty books of monstrous mayhem, ghostly frights and newfound terrors. Some of his bestselling books include the critically acclaimed *Creature, They Rise,* and *The Montauk Monster,* the nostalgic *Money Back Guaranteed* series, and *Jessica Backman's Death in the Afterlife* trilogy.

He can be heard and seen on his two long-running podcasts, "Final Guys" and "Monster Men".

He's a father, husband, cat owner (aren't all horror writers?), pizza and beer lover, and a battle-scarred Mets fan. He lived with the ghost of a young boy for 25 years, was part of a mass UFO sighting in the 80s, and is still waiting for Bigfoot to show up in his yard.

www.huntershea.com